Tomorrow's Dream

JANETTE OKE & T. DAVIS BUNN

Tomorrow's Dream

JO

Tomorrow's Dream
A Literary Express, Inc. Book
(a subsidiary of Doubleday Direct, Inc.)
Reprinted by special arrangement with:
Bethany House Publishers
A Ministry of Bethany Fellowship, Inc.
11300 Hampshire Avenue South
Minneapolis, Minnesota 55438

PRINTING HISTORY
A Bethany House Publication / June 1998
The Janette Oke Collection / 1998

If you would be interested in purchasing additional copies of this
book, please write to this address for information:

The Janette Oke Collection
1540 Broadway
New York, NY 10036

ISBN: 1-58165-073-6

Printed in the United States of America

This book is dedicated to

William Melvin Bunn

In Loving Memory

JANETTE OKE was born in Champion, Alberta, during the depression years, to a Canadian prairie farmer and his wife. She is a graduate of Mountain View Bible College in Didsbury, Alberta, where she met her husband, Edward. They were married in May of 1957, and went on to pastor churches in Indiana as well as Calgary and Edmonton, Canada.

The Okes have three sons and one daughter and are enjoying the addition of grandchildren to the family. Edward and Janette have both been active in their local church, serving in various capacities as Sunday school teachers and board members. They make their home near Calgary, Alberta.

T. DAVIS BUNN, a native of North Carolina, is a former international business executive whose career has taken him to over forty countries in Europe, Africa, and the Middle East. With topics as diverse as romance, history, and intrigue, Bunn's books continue to reach readers of all ages and interests. He was recently named Novelist In Residence at Regent's Park College, Oxford University. He and his wife, Isabella, currently reside not far from that historic town.

Tomorrow's Dream

CHAPTER ONE

KYLE COULD NOT HELP but pause and gaze at her reflection. The hall mirror was at the bottom of the stairs, and she told herself that she needed to stop a moment and catch her breath. Which of course was silly, particularly since she was descending the stairway. But it was something pregnant women did—they stopped and caught their breath. She had heard it all her life, and it suited the moment perfectly. No matter that she had never felt better. Or happier. She was five months along, and she had every right to stop and catch her breath if she wanted. Even to smile in appreciation into the mirror.

The mirror was a present from Abigail, Kyle's adoptive mother, and it was one of the most elaborate items she and Kenneth had in their home. Abigail's tastes tended toward the extravagant, and the full-length mirror in its gilded frame overpowered their little Georgetown row house. Abigail checked her appearance in it every time she arrived or departed, usually making some comment about how different this dwelling was from the estate on which Kyle had been raised. Or how nice it would be to see this hanging in a larger entryway. Kenneth tended to sigh a lot whenever

Abigail came for a visit. And Kyle went back and forth between exasperation and amusement.

Kyle loved their little home. Almost too small to be called a house, it was connected on either side to dwellings just like it—three-story wooden structures dating back to a time when Georgetown was a middle-class community in the nation's capital, rather than the newest desirable neighborhood of Washington, D.C. So much was changing as the nation approached the middle of the decade, as though the sixties had determined to redefine everything and everybody. Even here.

Kyle thought their home was like a dollhouse, her girlhood dreams come true. It was tiny and perfect and set on a leafy street not far from the shops and the university. Everybody walked or biked in Georgetown. It was a place full of young people and interesting things. Plus, it was the nicest neighborhood within easy distance of her recently discovered brother, Joel. And it was only a quick bus ride or a long walk to Kenneth's office in the Rothmore Insurance Building. The time he would have spent commuting was free now to help Joel out with his mission to the homeless and hopeless of society.

The thought of her brother caused Kyle to look down at the envelope with the wedding announcement in her hand. Finally, he had asked Ruthie to marry him.

Thinking of the young couple brought another smile to Kyle's lips. Joel's heart condition had made him reluctant to burden Ruthie with the uncertain future that marriage to him would mean. But she loved him with a steadfastness that simply would not accept his assessment. She had left her secure world at the Miller farm and joined his inner-city ministry. There she faithfully worked beside him, supporting him, loving him, sharing his triumphs and his disappointments. Silently she made him realize that she asked for nothing more than to be a part of his life. Of his work. Her patience had finally brought him to accept what her heart had been saying. Joel and she were to be married.

In Kyle's happiness she could almost forget that Joel had a heart condition, that his life hung by the slenderest of threads. He had lived far longer than any doctor had predicted—so why not for another ten, twenty, forty years? But this was not the argument that had won him over and finally prompted him to propose marriage. Joel had already learned to live without giving much thought to the morrow, something which Kyle found quite astonishing, as her own dreams were so full of her joy over the future.

Joel had finally accepted Ruthie's words as truth, that whatever days were left to them she wanted to spend together, as husband and wife, that she was willing to give her own future over to the Lord their God. It had been hard for Joel, very hard. Watching him come to terms with his own feelings and the worst of his fears had taught Kyle a great deal about this brother she hardly knew. Joel had never been afraid for himself. Yet allowing himself to love Ruthie had forced him to ache for what was yet to come.

Kyle looked at her reflection once more. What really brought the sparkle to her eyes and the joy to her heart was yesterday's report from her doctor. Everything was going well with her pregnancy. In a very few months she and Kenneth were to become parents. Kyle had never felt so excited in all her life. It was almost too much joy to contain at one time. A baby. Their own child. Hers and Kenneth's. Something so beautiful to share. So completely theirs. A precious entrustment from God. It was going to be very difficult to wait through the remaining days. Difficult, yet full of exquisite pleasure.

She turned sideways so the bulge was more evident in the mirror and caressed her abdomen with the hand holding the invitation. Her baby had been moving a lot that morning, as though impatient to be out and about with the family. The thought was enough to send another shiver of joy through her frame. Kyle's expression, even when she was not smiling, shone with delight over the promise of all that was to come.

Her gaze fell on the Bible, still open on the table by the rocking chair. She spoke aloud the underlined words from Psalm 100, which she had read earlier: "For the Lord is good; his mercy is everlasting, and his truth endureth to all generations."

Kyle felt her heart would surely explode with love— for God, for Kenneth, for the small person within her. She thought she could actually feel God's love embracing her, holding her close, warming her with His smile.

The clock on the living room mantel struck the hour, a reminder that sent her scurrying for her hat and coat and keys. She stepped through the front door, took a deep breath of the fall-laden air, and decided that she would walk after all. She would be a few minutes late, but the doctor had urged her to walk as much as she could manage. And it was a beautiful day, truly filled with all the promise that one future could hold.

Her watch said she was ten minutes late when Kyle entered the Mayflower Hotel's main restaurant. Yet not even the sight of Kenneth's slightly exasperated glance could dim her smile. She hurried over, pulling off her coat and hat to settle them on a free chair. "Sorry I'm late," she said to the two already seated.

"No you're not," said Abigail sharply. "You're clearly

delighted to have caused us to sit here and fume in impatience." But even her mother's crossness was no match for Kyle's exuberance. Abigail turned a smooth cheek to accept her adopted daughter's kiss, then studied her face. "You look—well, positively radiant."

"Thank you, Mother." Though she had lived through the discovery of her adoption and had met her birth parents, Kyle still called Abigail "mother." "You are beautiful as always," she said warmly.

"Nonsense. I'm getting older every day. Age and beauty do not mix. You'll find that out soon enough." She turned her face away in disapproval as Kyle leaned over, caressed Kenneth's cheek, and kissed him gently. Abigail did not care for public displays of affection.

Kenneth ignored Abigail's displeasure from across the table, smiled up at his wife, and said, "Apology accepted."

"Really," noted Abigail, "I fail to see why you two find it necessary to show such sentiment in public. It's simply not done."

Kyle slid into the chair between them, took her husband's hand, and cradled it in her lap. "It is by us."

"Hmph. Well, anyway, we've got to get you some clothes. You're not a college girl anymore, Kyle."

"I think she looks lovely," Kenneth chided. Granted, her oversized cable-knit sweater had been borrowed from Kenneth's side of the closet, but her own things were getting a bit tight for her.

Kyle gentled her husband with a squeeze to his hand and quipped, "In case you haven't noticed, Mother, I *am* five months pregnant."

"Of course I've noticed. Everyone's noticed. How could they not when you insist on wearing—"

"Mother." Kyle said the one word very quietly, but her tone was firm enough to silence even Abigail. Kenneth

15

glanced her way and caught her eye with a quick nod of approval.

Kyle turned back to her mother and asked, "Have you decided about attending Joel's wedding?"

Abigail folded and unfolded her napkin before replying, "Oh, all right. I suppose it's the best thing, really."

"Oh, that's wonderful." Kyle released Kenneth's hand to give Abigail a hug. "Did you pray about it like I suggested?"

"Yes, a little, although I can't say I had much of an answer. I find it difficult to understand why God would want to involve himself in such mundane affairs."

"Oh yes, Mother, He does! Remember the Scripture that tells us He knows when a sparrow falls from a tree? And isn't my brother's wedding more important than that? I do think God cares about it and wants you to come." Kyle beamed at the precise woman seated across from her. "This is wonderful. I'm so glad you're becoming friends with my other family."

"So am I," Kenneth allowed quietly.

"I must confess that they are quite nice people, especially Harry." Abigail seemed to compress her lips to hide a smile. "Although what we have in common I cannot possibly imagine."

"You have me in common," Kyle gaily declared. Then turning to the approaching waiter, she went on, "I am positively starving. I'll have your daily special."

"Make that two," Kenneth said.

"A green salad," Abigail ordered, "with the dressing on the side." She turned back to her daughter to say, "Really, Kyle, wouldn't it be wise to watch your weight a little more?"

"I can't. I'm hungry all the time."

"She'll finish her meal and have half of mine, you watch," Kenneth joked.

"The doctor says a healthy appetite is good for the baby, Mother."

"It may be, but you just wait and see what it's like trying to get the pounds off after." Abigail stared back at the two faces across the table and raised one hand. "All right, I'll stop. I can see my advice counts for nothing here."

"You are always welcome to offer advice," Kyle said briskly, determined not to allow Abigail to dampen her mood. She fished in her purse and brought out the wedding invitation. "Look what arrived today."

Kenneth accepted the envelope and studied the pen-and-ink sketch of Joel's mission house. As he handed it to Abigail his features reflected the concern they all shared over Joel's heart condition. "I hope they're doing the right thing."

"They are," Kyle insisted, happy for Ruthie, wanting everyone to have all their dreams come true as hers were.

Abigail glanced briefly at the wedding invitation. "It will be another of those simple affairs, I imagine."

"Yes, and you know how much you enjoyed our wedding," Kyle reminded her, sharing a grin with her husband.

"I still say you deserved a big society wedding, and it would have been marvelous to plan." Then Abigail's face softened at the memory of the event. "But, yes, it was quite delightful in its own way."

Kyle gave her husband's hand another squeeze. They had insisted on having their wedding at Kenneth's church, which had now become their church home. It had been a quiet and modest affair, but full of shared joy with family and dear friends.

Abigail straightened herself back into her habitual demeanor. "Which reminds me, Kyle. We were just discussing something of vital importance before you arrived."

One glance at Kenneth's face was enough to tell Kyle what it was. "Not the church, Mother. Not again."

"Yes, again. I simply fail to see why we cannot attend church downtown together."

"Our own church supports Joel's mission fellowship," Kenneth reminded her. "Not to mention being the church I have attended since arriving in Washington."

"All the family attends our church except you," Kyle added. "And we would love to——"

"I would not be happy there and you know it. Not a single member of our circle of friends goes there. Whereas you have known our church all your life."

Kyle did not mention that her mother had not begun attending church until just a few short months ago. Nor that the only times she had herself entered the large city church were for several gala weddings and her adoptive father's funeral. "We are very happy where we are," she stated calmly.

"Well, if you won't do it for me, do it for your husband. Think of all the excellent connections Kenneth would make there. Not to mention raising your child in the proper environment."

"We do not attend church for the sake of business connections," Kenneth said. The only signal that his patience was wearing thin was a softer tone. "We attend church to worship our Lord."

Kyle glanced from one to the other, feeling the lines of tension gradually drawing tighter across the table. Business was a touchy subject between her husband and her mother, and adding religion made for an explosive combination.

Lawrence Rothmore's legacy meant that Kyle now controlled a majority of stock in the Rothmore Insurance

Company. Kenneth had been employed there for some years and, under Lawrence's tutelage, had risen quickly to a place of responsibility in the company. But the board remained unconvinced that the entire company should be placed in the hands of such a young and untested executive. To have insisted on Kenneth being given the role of chief executive would have cost them many of their large corporate clients, as they would have departed with the disgruntled board members. Besides, Kenneth had explained, holding the position of executive vice-president for several years was not necessarily a bad thing.

"You can most certainly worship God just as well downtown with me," Abigail retorted, "and do your career worlds of good at the same time."

Kenneth started to speak, then paused for the waiter to set down their plates. Kyle used the diversion as a chance to place her hand on Kenneth's arm. When he turned her way, she gave her head a minute shake. When Abigail's attention returned to their conversation, Kyle said firmly, "Mother, we are going to attend our own church. You are welcome to come with us whenever you like. We will be happy to join you from time to time, but our church home will remain exactly where it is."

"But——"

"The matter is closed," Kyle said, firmness returning to her voice.

Looking at her husband, Kyle asked, "Would you say the blessing for us?"

CHAPTER TWO

KYLE TURNED TO WHERE her birth parents beamed from the corner of the church's front entryway. "How do I look?" she asked.

Martha Grimes regarded her with eyes threatening to overflow at any moment. "You look wonderful, daughter."

"And big," Harry Grimes added with a grin. "Bigger and happier with every passing day."

"She does not. She looks wonderful."

Harry asked, "How close is it now?"

"Nine weeks, but the doctor thinks I might be a little early."

"I don't know, I have this feeling it's going to be a girl," Martha announced.

"Don't say that anywhere near Abigail," Kyle warned. "She is absolutely positive it's going to be a boy."

"Oh, pshaw, what does she know?"

"As much as you do," Harry reminded his wife.

Kenneth joined the little group. He and Harry both wore the sprig of flowers in their lapels indicating that they were groomsmen in the wedding and were also ushering guests to their places. Joel had told his father there was no one else he would choose for his best man. Kenneth quipped, "I thought there were supposed to be two of us working here."

"You're doing such a good job," Harry replied, "I felt like I should just stand back and watch a master at work."

"You did not. You're just being lazy." Martha shook her head in mock scolding. "Shame on you."

"Somebody needs to stand here and hold this wall up," Harry replied.

"Everybody watch out," Kenneth said with a little smile, adjusting his tie. "Here comes—"

"Stop it now," Martha reproved gently, then turned her smile in the direction of the outer stairs. "Hello, Abigail."

Abigail stepped in from the brilliant winter sunlight and had to stop and blink several times. "Oh, hello, everyone. Is this the welcoming committee?"

"Reinforcements," Kenneth agreed with a straight face.

Kyle nudged him and stepped forward to give Abigail a hug. The woman wore a stunning outfit of midnight blue set off with a string of cultured pearls. "You look wonderful."

"Thank you. And you look quite—enormous." She frowned as she rubbed the fabric of Kyle's dress between thumb and forefinger. "I distinctly remember telling the seamstress I wanted your dress done in silk."

Martha's meaningful look drew Harry from propping up the side wall. "Come on, Abigail, we're holding up traffic here." He crooked his arm and said, "Mind if I escort the most beautiful lady here to her place?"

She took his arm and said, "Harry Grimes, don't you dare start on me today. You know what I think about weddings."

"Now, let's see." Harry craned his neck up and down the church, a mischievous grin on his face. "We've got to set you behind a column or something so you don't upstage the bride."

"This is your final warning." But Abigail was struggling to keep her smile under wraps. She pointed down the center aisle. "There. Right up there in the middle. That's where I'm sitting."

Kyle waited for them to move off before saying to her husband, "Why can't you be like that with Abigail?"

"I would," Kenneth replied, "if I could only figure out how he does it."

"That's easy," Martha Grimes responded. "Harry has had a lifetime's experience with dark moods. He's now found a way to put them to good use."

Kenneth nodded slowly. "That proves just how much better a man Harry is than me."

"Oh, you—it isn't *that* hard." But Kyle had to smile. The day was just too wonderful, the miracles too abundant. All her family were gathered and happy, friendly and chatting, as families were supposed to be. "Where's Sarah?"

"She's coming with the rest of the Millers." Ruthie's younger sister was to be the other bridesmaid. Kenneth glanced at his watch. "I sure hope they get here before the bride."

"Joel's gone to fetch them," Martha said. "He insisted. Said he wanted to be the one to host them here. All but Mother Ruth. She's coming with her daughter."

The pastor slipped in through the side door. He shared a smile with everyone and a handshake with Kenneth. "Everything all right?"

"It will be," Kenneth replied. "Just as soon as the bride and groom arrive."

"Always helps to have them around for a wedding," the pastor agreed. Patrick Langdon was more than the pastor of their church. He was a friend. He had accepted Joel's mission idea and presented it to the church, then helped arrange for the project to be housed in a derelict warehouse owned by a parishioner. Joel and Ruthie had been busy for months turning the top floor into an apartment. Patrick smiled at Kyle. "You look happy enough for it to be your own wedding day."

"I'm so glad for Joel and Ruthie," Kyle replied.

He glanced at his watch. "Well, let's hope they get here in time."

"They'll be here."

"Then I suppose I'd better get myself ready." He smiled at the next group of people coming in through the doors, patted Kenneth's arm, and moved off.

Kyle listened to the talk swirl, watching one person after another climb the stairs and exchange greetings and be shown to their seat. All these people from church, new friends and old, sponsors of the mission fellowship, even some of the young people Joel and Ruthie had helped bring off the streets. So much joy, it seemed to Kyle, that the church roof would have to lift off just to hold it all.

She glanced down at her dress. She had indeed gone to Abigail's dressmaker. But she had ordered the seamstress to use a delicate chintz for her bridesmaid's dress, not silk. Kyle wanted a dress that would help her fit into the background. This was to be Ruthie's day. Ruthie's and Joel's.

Kyle recalled the concern the couple had felt over their decision to be married in Washington. Ruthie was not giving up her Mennonite heritage. But she was working with street people, the flower children who were flooding the nation's capital. Dropping out—that was a term they heard more often each day, some of them dropping until they hit rock bottom. For some at least the mission was becoming a lifeline, a last hope.

"Morning Glory" was the name of Joel's project in the

Adams-Morgan district of Washington, D.C. The mission was growing bigger all the time, with more young people arriving every day. Joel remained a gentle beacon, while his name and that of the center were passed by word of mouth all over the eastern seaboard.

Joel and Ruthie had made a wonderful team even before the decision to marry. Her personal warmth and caring nature created an atmosphere of trust for the frightened and often suspicious teenagers who found their way to the mission.

It had been hard for Ruthie to go home and tell her parents they would not see their eldest daughter married in traditional Mennonite fashion. But Ruthie and Joel had found a genuine home in this Georgetown church, and Ruthie had wanted it to be the place where she was wed. Kyle had joined Joel in praying for peace and understanding the entire time Ruthie was home. To their surprise there had been no arguments, no quarrels. Instead, Mrs. Miller had risen as soon as her daughter had finished her explanation and had given her a fierce hug. Then she had said that perhaps it would be nice if they made a wedding dress together—a design that would incorporate the simple lines of their traditional dress but with a fabric that would be in keeping with her new life.

Martha's cry of, "Joel is here!" caused a rush from the vestibule to the front doorway and outside as the mission van's doors sprang open. Kyle felt a moment's pang as she stood there watching the Miller family pile out. The past two years had been very hard for them, as it had for the entire Mennonite farming community. Every conversation with Joel and Ruthie seemed to bring with it more bad news. Recently there had even been some talk about selling a tract of farmland that had been in the Miller household for five generations. Kyle hurriedly pushed those thoughts and concerns away. Today was intended for nothing except joy.

Sarah, Ruthie's younger sister, wore a lovely frock whose homespun simplicity softened and adorned the strong farm girl in a way that no store-bought dress ever could. Her head was covered by a small ivory-colored veil, as was Kyle's, both hand stitched by Mrs. Miller and representing many hours of work.

The boys came tumbling out, Simon and Garth and young Jacob, all in their best dark suits and work boots polished until they gleamed. Last of all, Mr. Miller eased his way from the front seat, settling his crutch in place and turning to the church to give them all a smile and a wave.

Mr. Miller made his way up the stairs, pausing halfway to point at Kyle and proclaim, "Look at her, is she not beautiful as the day?"

"Shah, Papa, not so loud." But Simon's eyes were on Kyle as well. "A good morning to you, Missus. It is grand to see you so happy."

"Yah, yah, what I say." Mr. Miller climbed the remaining stairs, his crutch and missing limb not slowing him at all. He stopped to tower over Kyle, his beard more silver than black now, but his voice was as strong as the hand that settled on her shoulder. "I am thinking maybe the sun is rising in your eyes."

Kyle blushed as she put her own hand on top of his. "Today I am so full of two happinesses, I think I can't hold them both. I was so afraid this day would never come."

"You and all the family." He turned to where Joel had parked the van and was now making his way up the stairs toward them. "Yah, that Choel, he run from the altar like a deer from——"

"Papa," Sarah chided, coming up alongside them. "Better we sit ourselves down and pray for the wedding couple."

"A good idea, my daughter has." The hand rose and fell again on Kyle's shoulder. "Health and happiness, full measures of both, pressed down and flowing over."

Kyle turned back to watch her brother come bounding up the church stairs. There was no indication of ill health that day, not in his beaming face or in the excited energy which filled his spare frame. *My brother.* Two years ago she had first learned of his existence, and still the very word sent a thrill of joy through her.

Kyle drew back inside the church entryway with a little shiver. The morning frost had been melted away by the brilliant sunlight, but she could still feel the fresh winter chill.

Joel entered the church's outer doors, walked straight over and gave Kyle a hug. She had to laugh. Simple gestures still came hard between them, but today there was no room for either confusion or reserve.

Joel leaned back. "Sorry, did I squeeze too hard, little mother?"

"The baby's fine and so am I." She pulled him back for a second hug before releasing him with another laugh. "Blessings on you and on this day, my brother."

The Millers' arrival was causing quite a stir among the gathering. Kyle watched the big man proudly lead his boys down to the second row. Simon waited until his father was seated, then placed his wide-brimmed hat on the pew and went over to sit alongside Joel on the front row.

Only Sarah remained behind with Kyle in the vestibule.

"All night I spent," she whispered. "All night long I prayed for Ruthie and Joel. I am so glad for them and their new life together."

"Ruthie has been the happiest person in the whole world since Joel agreed to the marriage," Kyle replied.

"You too, you are happy this day."

"Happy for all of us." And then, "Oh-h."

Kenneth was instantly by her side. "Are you all right?"

She managed a wobbly smile for her husband. "I'm . . . I'm fine. Maybe the baby just kicked a nerve or something—"

"Here they are now!" Sarah pointed out to where a car had pulled up in front of the church.

"I'd better go sit down," Martha Grimes said, tugging on her husband's arm. "Stand up straight, now. Make your son proud."

Kenneth turned back to search Kyle's face. "Are you all right?" he asked again.

"Oh yes, truly it was nothing. I'm just fine." She squeezed Kenneth's hand on her arm and turned to watch the bride coming up the walk.

"Oh, Ruthie, she is so beautiful." There was a catch in Sarah's voice. "And so happy."

Kyle understood what was behind Sarah's worry. "Be happy for her."

"Yes, of course, you speak rightly." Sarah took a shaky breath and straightened her shoulders. "This is her day. I must show joy for her and give the morrow over to our Lord."

Ruthie's dress was a work of love. Her sturdy frame was made lithe and delicate by the simple lines and white muslin and organdy folds. The sides and back and veil were embroidered with little cream-colored flowers, and it looked as though the coming spring cascaded and flowed with her every step.

Inside the vestibule there was excited whispering. Kenneth offered Mother Ruth his arm.

Mother and daughter first exchanged a long hug, and unshed tears gathered in all the watching eyes. Such joy, such fear, such hope. The combination of emotions filled the air in the vestibule.

Through a crack in the door, the bridal party watched Kenneth seat Mrs. Miller by her husband. As he hurried back to join the bridal party, the church rustled, full of quiet anticipation, like a forest of trees on tiptoe waiting to catch a coming breeze.

Kenneth paused until the two bridesmaids had straightened the back of Ruthie's dress and taken up their bouquets, then gave Harry the nod.

Together Harry and Kenneth drew open the double doors. The organist had been waiting for that signal and began with a pair of loud chords to alert the congregation.

Joel and Simon rose from their places at the front and went to stand beside the waiting minister. The wedding march began, and Ruthie took her first step into the sanctuary. She seemed to float down the aisle, held aloft by the power and the joy which beamed from both her own face and from Joel's. Kyle moved up the aisle behind her, watching the light in Joel's features grow with each step Ruthie took.

Ruthie handed Kyle her bouquet, then turned to look into the face of her beloved Joel. Joel took her arm and stood in front of the minister.

Then Kyle and all the congregation watched as the light the two of them had brought was joined into one.

CHAPTER THREE

"KYLE? HONEY?"

She struggled to open her eyes. For some reason, that simple effort cost her dearly. Kyle focused upon Kenneth's face hovering above her. Worry lines creased his forehead. "How long have I been asleep?" she murmured.

"I don't know. A while." He reached down and helped her straighten up. She had slid down the couch until she half sat, half lay with her back twisted unnaturally. "That can't be comfortable. Let me help you upstairs."

"All right." But rising was an effort, even with him there to support her. The baby had grown until her abdomen felt tight as a drum, and the weight seemed to bear down on her. She stifled a groan as her back muscles tightened in complaint over having lain crooked for too long.

"Just lean on me."

She did. It was the only way to rise. Kyle pressed one hand into the small of her back as she moved with him toward the stairs. "How can I sleep so long and still wake up tired?"

"Did you ask the doctor?"

"Yes. He said it was because I was sleeping for two now."

"That doesn't sound like much of an answer."

"It was just his way of telling me not to worry. And you." Kyle gave her husband a smile. "It won't be long now."

"I hope not. You're already a week overdue."

As if she had not been aware of that fact every minute of those seven days. But Kyle did not say it. Kenneth did not need another reason to worry. "I never knew it was possible to get this big," she said ruefully.

He reached the top of the stairs and paused a moment to let her rest from the climb. "Would you like to take a bath? That always helps you feel better."

"No, I think . . ."

Kenneth stood and held her arm as she bent over slowly, almost collapsing in on herself. She eased back up in careful stages, taking a series of quick panting breaths. His worry lines had deepened with sudden fear. "Honey, what's the matter?"

She turned and gave him the bravest smile she could manage. "I think it's time."

Kyle stirred restlessly in her sleep, dimly aware that she was in some way not the same person who had opened her eyes to yesterday's dawn. As consciousness returned she realized what that difference was. She was a mother. A mother. At long last she had been granted the desire of her heart. They had a son. A precious, beautiful baby boy. Born during the long, dark hours of the previous night. Kenneth had laid his cheek against her flushed, damp forehead, and they had cried and prayed together. A son, already bearing a name. Charles Kenneth Adams. She could not wait to see him again. To hold him. To cradle him close to her heart.

Nor could she wait for others to see him. Martha and Harry would be so pleased. And Abigail. This beautiful child was bound to bring a smile even to Abigail's features. And Joel. His first nephew. He so loved the little ones. He would welcome this baby boy with the overflowing of his love-filled, ailing heart.

"I can't wait to show him off to Maggie," Kyle whispered to herself, thinking of the housekeeper who had loved her and raised her since infancy. And Bertrand, her husband. They had retired to a cottage down on the Maryland coast. Kyle smiled at the thought of the straitlaced old gentleman getting down on his hands and knees to play with the baby.

Kyle stirred again. She listened to the tread of nurses in the hall. Soft words of greeting came as they good-naturedly gave news of the night and placed bundled babies into eager arms. "He slept like a top," or, "She's been impatient to get to Mommy."

Kyle smiled. Soon they would be bringing her little Charles. Soon she would get to hold him. She chafed with anticipation, especially now that the ether which had gentled the birthing process was gradually leaving her system. Soon she would count his toes and fingers and see if he had his daddy's eyes or his grandfather Harry's strong chin. She could hardly wait.

But each pair of footsteps continued past her door. Impatience soon had her again stirring restlessly. It was so difficult to lie there and wait, while the soft murmurs of other mothers reached her as they cuddled and nursed their own infants. She would have sprung from the bed and searched down the long hall had she not been given strict orders to stay where she was.

When the waiting was almost unbearable, a nurse appeared at her door. She gave a cheery smile and announced, "Mrs. Adams, I've brought your son to say good morning."

But it was not as Kyle had expected. The woman in her crisp white uniform leaned over the bed but did not offer Kyle the baby. Instead her arms still firmly grasped the blue-blanketed bundle.

As disappointment and confusion swept through her, Kyle reached out a tentative hand and gently eased a finger into the curled fist of her little boy. His small hand felt cold to her touch. His eyes did not open.

"You get some rest now." The nurse gave another brief smile and moved away from Kyle's bed.

But I want to hold him, Kyle's heart cried out. Instead she let the tiny hand slip from her fingers. As she watched the nurse depart with her son, she nearly wept.

Was this the usual hospital procedure? Were babies kept apart from their mothers after delivery? She didn't know. She had never gone through the experience before. Kyle felt confused and very unsettled, and wondered vaguely if perhaps her medication had not yet worn off. She lay back onto her pillows, eyes searching the empty doorway. She would have to wait. It was not her turn yet. But how could she ever endure more long hours without holding her son?

Her longing was so intense that her eyes burned and her throat filled. Kyle fought against a rising sense of rebellion over the unfairness. She willed herself to relax upon the hard white surface of the unyielding hospital bed.

CHAPTER FOUR

ONCE AGAIN KYLE OPENED her eyes to find Kenneth bending over her. Surprised, she glanced toward the window to measure the hour. "Is it already time?"

He settled his hand upon her shoulder. "Time for what?"

"Visiting hours. I can't believe I slept the entire day."

"It's ten."

"In the morning?"

"Yes."

Kyle shook her head. Now she was totally confused. "But visiting hours aren't until two."

Kenneth nodded. For the first time she looked closely into his face. His smile looked a bit forced. A shadow seemed to darken his eyes. Kyle pushed sudden fear away. Perhaps he was as impatient to get acquainted with their son as she was. The waiting was so difficult.

"Did they let you see him?" she asked.

"Yes . . . yes, I saw him after he was born. But I haven't seen him . . . today yet."

"It makes me a little upset. After all, he is our baby. I don't know why they feel they need to . . ." Kyle tried to rise into a sitting position. It was not at all comfortable, so she lay back down. "Isn't he beautiful? I saw him this morning. The nurse brought him in. If only they'd let me—"

"Kyle," Kenneth's tone stopped her. "The doctor asked me to come in this morning. He says . . . he needs to talk to us together."

Kyle's eyes widened. "What about?"

"I don't know. He wouldn't say. Except . . ." The shadows in Kenneth's eyes deepened and darkened, causing her joy to drain away. "The doctor just said that little Charles . . . well, has him concerned."

Fear gripped her throat and allowed nothing but an echo of his word. "Concerned?"

He took her hand, and his lips smiled, but his gaze did not ease. "I'm sure it's nothing to worry about. Some little thing that needs attention."

She grasped at the words as she did his hand, because she had to. She forced herself to take a deep breath. "Of course. He's big. And healthy. I saw for myself. Whatever it is, it can't be too serious."

The words buoyed her up, as though by saying them she could make so. Kyle went on, "Just think, in a few days we'll be going home. Our baby and us. I can't wait."

Her thoughts quickly turned to the waiting nursery. It was the one part of their modest home that she had furnished with little thought as to the cost. Kenneth had smiled in good-natured indulgence as she had insisted upon every possible convenience or extravagance for their new baby. Now the room was waiting. Blue and beckoning, for Kyle had secretly agreed with Abigail from the beginning that the child was going to be a boy.

Kenneth nodded in agreement to her words, but his answering smile never reached his eyes.

Footfalls in the hallway brought their attention to the door. But when Dr. Pearce appeared, he did not enter the room alone. Three figures followed closely on one another's heels.

The nurse led the way, carrying an official metal clipboard before her like a shield. Their family doctor followed behind, his gold-rimmed spectacles riding low on a long, pinched nose, his hair the usual disarray of sparse gray curls.

The man who walked at his side was in direct contrast to their comforting family doctor. He was young and intensely focused. In his stark white hospital coat and sharply creased trousers, he looked both important and foreboding. His presence in her room made Kyle feel even more uncomfortable.

"I asked Dr. Saunders to join us," Dr. Pearce said in his kindly, tired voice. "He is a pediatric surgeon."

Surgeon? Why? Kyle wanted to ask what he was doing here but could not form the words.

In spite of hospital protocol, Dr. Pearce seated himself on the edge of Kyle's bed. He nodded to Kenneth and said, "Son, why don't you grab yourself a chair."

Kenneth glanced to where the chair stood on the far wall and settled his arm on Kyle's shoulder. "Thanks, but I'm fine where I am."

The doctor nodded his understanding. He took a deep breath, as if seeking to draw strength from outside himself. "Kyle," he began slowly, "we're having a little problem with your baby."

Kyle felt her whole body freeze. The entire world

seemed to seize up tight. *Oh, dear God* was her inner whisper, just a short heart-wrenching prayer for what she did not understand.

"I was called back in by the staff a short time after his delivery. He wasn't getting his color the way they liked. I returned and had a look." He hesitated again.

The moments crawled like hours as Kyle waited, lying there helpless, holding her breath.

"I am not sure yet exactly why, but his heart does not seem to be functioning as it should."

Kyle groped blindly for Kenneth's hand and clutched at it with all her might.

"I called in Dr. Saunders. He's, well . . ." Again the hesitation, the searching breath. "The tests are all preliminary at this stage, you understand. But he, too, believes the boy might have some kind of heart condition."

The young doctor stepped forward. Kyle tore her eyes away from Dr. Pearce's face to look at him. He did not seem quite as distant and official as he had at first. Kyle read compassion in his eyes. When he spoke, his voice was soft, yet there was a strength and certainty to his tone that made his words pierce her very soul.

"We often have great success with corrective surgery," he began.

Kyle heard the consoling tone but could not understand. Her grip on Kenneth's hand tightened until her arm trembled with the strain. Surgery? Surgery for her baby boy? That was unthinkable. What were they talking about? She had seen him. He was fine. Why. . . ?

They were talking on. Kenneth was the only one who seemed able to listen. Kyle looked up and saw him nod, a strained and fearful expression on his face.

"Of course we will need more tests to determine the extent of damage," she heard the young doctor say through her haze of disbelief.

Was this some bad dream? Was she still under the influence of the anesthetic? Oh, if she could only force herself to wake up and make it all go away!

She heard Kenneth ask, "When?"

"I'd like to get a number of the tests done as quickly as possible." Dr. Saunders addressed his matter-of-fact words directly to Kenneth now, as though aware that only he was able to comprehend what was being said. "Time is of the utmost importance in such cases. We'll need you to sign the releases before we can proceed. That's why we called you in this morning."

"Releases for the surgery?" Kyle noted that Kenneth's voice was so hoarse and strained it did not even sound like her husband.

"No. No, we won't be able to do surgery at this point. The baby is not strong enough yet . . . he's really not strong enough." The strain now seemed to touch the young doctor as his words began to push out, rushing toward what was hardest to say. "Right now we are devoting all our efforts to keeping him with us. By the time he has strengthened and grown a bit we should know the full extent of the damage. Once that's been assessed, then we can look at the feasibility of surgery." He paused, looking relieved now that the worst was out in the open. "The releases are necessary for our tests."

But Kenneth was not going to let him off that easily. "I don't understand. If there need to be tests, then why not just go ahead and do them?"

Old Dr. Pearce looked at Kenneth, then Kyle, pain in his eyes. He rubbed a tired hand through his remaining hair. "It is possible," he said, clearly hating the words he needed to speak, "that we might lose such a fragile baby in the process of assessment."

Kyle clenched her eyes shut with the same vehemence that she squeezed on Kenneth's hand. *No. No. It isn't possible. Not little Charles. I won't have it. You can't do the tests. You can't.*

But Kenneth was speaking again. "And if the tests aren't done?"

When there was only silence in response, Kyle forced herself to open her eyes. The old doctor sat there beside her, slowly shaking his head. "Son, we wouldn't even think of doing them unless they were absolutely essential. If we don't go ahead, your child has no chance of survival at all. We'd have nowhere near enough knowledge as to how to proceed with treatment."

Kenneth opened his mouth, closed it, then tried again, forcing out words so heavy they dropped like stones from heaven. "And if you do the tests? What are our chances then?"

Dr. Saunders started to speak, but Dr. Pearce raised his gaze in time to halt the younger man with one quick look. The silence in the room hung like a shroud until Dr. Pearce finally said, "We'll know more after the tests."

Kenneth nodded, his face bleached white, his jaw stiff.

The nurse pushed her metal pad toward him, pointing at the places where he needed to sign. Without a word Kenneth accepted the pen and wrote on the indicated line.

No, Kyle wished to scream. *Don't sign it.* But instead of speaking, she turned her face into the stack of pillows and began to sob, her shoulders heaving with the intensity of her pain.

"Kyle." She heard the doctor's fatherly tone. "Nurse Jacobs has a little needle for you. It will help you get some sleep."

Kyle was only slightly aware of the hands upon her arm and Kenneth's voice speaking to her from some grim distance somewhere.

"It's going to be all right, darling. God will see us through this. Hang on. Just hang on."

Hang on, Kyle repeated to herself. Of course. God would see them through.

CHAPTER FIVE

THE TELEPHONE'S RING jarred the silence of their empty little house. Kyle rushed toward the hall phone, not so much because she wanted to speak with someone but because the sound did not belong. She lifted the receiver and said hello.

"Kyle, darling, it's Martha. How are you, dear?"

Kyle couldn't form an answer in her mind. She raised her head and flinched as she caught sight of her reflection in the mirror.

"It's been over a week since I've heard from you," Martha rushed on into the silence. "I had to call. Has there been any word?"

"No." She had to turn away from the hollowness in her eyes. But comfort was not to be found elsewhere. There should be a baby here. Every nook and cranny of her empty house shouted Charles Kenneth's absence. "No, nothing," she repeated.

"But it's been over a month now." Martha's voice rose. "How long do they need to finish these tests of theirs?"

"They can't tell us. They say they don't know yet." There should be a baby for her to lift from the crib upstairs,

43

a baby to hold and love and fit into her heart's barren space. A baby to fill the house with its light and cries and love. "They won't—can't tell us anything. And it's been six weeks, Martha. Six weeks tomorrow."

"Oh, my darling, Kyle, you sound so sad. Wait, Harry's telling me something." There was a murmuring in the background, then Martha said, "Harry suggests that we take you out for a drive. We could go have lunch in Annapolis and a walk along the Maryland shore. There won't be a soul out this time of year."

"Thank you, Martha. But I can't." Her slow revolution around the hall brought her back to her reflection in the mirror. There were new creases to her forehead, new shadows. Her gaze looked as dull and lifeless as her voice sounded to her own ears. "Abigail has arranged for baby Charles to be seen by one of the world's leading heart specialists—a doctor from the Mayo Clinic. He's here for a conference, and she pulled some strings."

"That's wonderful, dear." Martha's enthusiasm was full of hope and encouragement. "At last maybe you'll hear some good news. When is your meeting?"

"Kenneth is supposed to pick me up in a half hour." But saying her husband's name renewed the pain and the guilt she had been feeling all morning. It was so strong she had to let a little of it out. "We had a . . . well, a fight this morning."

"Oh no, I'm so sorry."

"It was my fault. Kenneth has been so strong, and I started arguing with him over nothing at all." There was a little catch to her voice, but she fought it off. It was easy to do. She had cried so much there was no need to shed any more tears. If tears could ease her worry or bring Charles home, it would have happened weeks ago. "I just don't see how he can get up and go to the office like . . . like nothing is wrong."

"But he has to go, dear. He has a job. The world doesn't stop because—"

"But it *should* stop." She heard the unreasonableness in her voice and did not care. She was not arguing with Martha. She was giving voice to the storm of feelings that robbed her nights of sleep and her days of meaning. She was calling out for the baby who was not there in her arms. "How *dare* people keep walking by outside my house. Or laugh. Or say hello to each other like nothing was the matter. How *dare* they."

Martha was silent a long moment before suggesting, "Maybe we should pray together."

"That's all I do." Kyle's gaze shifted from the mirror to the Bible resting on her little desk. She had tried to read it since her return from the hospital, but the words were as lifeless as her heart. She had given up even the attempt. She turned away. "I pray so hard I feel like I've wrung my heart dry."

"Well, we will keep praying right along with you, my darling. Both of us. Night and day. Just remember that."

"Thank you, Martha. I have to go now."

When Kyle hung up the phone and walked into the living room, the clock over the mantel seemed to mock her. The ticking slowed and slowed until time was frozen into the same endless void that was in her heart and her home. Kyle wrung her hands and willed the time to move forward until Kenneth would come and pick her up and they could go see her baby again.

Turning away from the clock and walking back into the hallway, Kyle picked up her coat and seated herself in the high-backed chair by the door. She stared through the narrow front window, wishing Kenneth's car would appear and she could open the door and walk away from the emptiness that was in her home. She glanced at her watch, held it to her ear, then sighed and let her hand drop back to her lap.

Kyle wished Martha had not called again. It was too hard to talk with her. It brought up too many things she would rather keep locked away inside. Where was Martha's God all those years when Martha's own baby daughter was missing from her arms? Where was Kyle's God now?

The tap on Kenneth's door had become a familiar sound over the past six weeks. "Am I disturbing you?" Abigail opened it a crack. "Are you ready?"

"Come on in." He pushed back in his chair. "I have one more letter to approve, and we can be on our way."

But instead of returning to the letter in front of him, he watched her enter, close the door, walk over, and sit down. Of all the traumas and stresses of the previous six weeks, nothing could have prepared him for the current situation with Abigail. The two of them were becoming friends. Not simply allies against the fear and the strain. Genuine friends. Abigail had the ability to say more with a lift of an eyebrow than most people could with an hour of words. And she knew the value of saying nothing at all, a quality he would never have expected to find in her. But it was there. And it had proven to be a powerful comfort.

Abigail asked, "How is my girl doing?"

"There are good days and bad days," Kenneth replied. "Today was a bad day."

"What happened?"

He shook his head and sighed the words, "This is killing her, Abigail. I can't blame her for what she said."

"Of course you can't." The normally proud features held a depth of feeling he would never have expected. "But it must still hurt terribly."

"I made the mistake of talking about business at the breakfast table this morning. I have a dozen things that have been put on hold since Charles was born, and I've got to move on them. I want her to know——"

"Don't tell her." Abigail was firm, decisive. "Just do it."

"It's her company."

"Not right now it's not," Abigail said. "Her world holds no space for anything but worry and grief."

He nodded. Her determined stance helped mightily and granted Kenneth the ability to accept what he had not wanted to see. "Abigail, I owe you an apology."

"Kenneth, there is absolutely no need——"

"Yes there is, and please let me say this." He stopped and took a breath, trying to ease the pressure building inside. "Ever since we first met, I have seen you as an adversary."

"And with good reason."

"Please, this is hard enough as it is," he said, raising a hand. "All my life I have read about showing the love of God to others. Forgiving the wrongful acts as God forgets and forgives our own sins. And here, with my own mother-in-law, I have held on to my own barriers." He had to stop there and breathe again. "I want to ask your forgiveness, Abigail."

"There is nothing to forgive."

"Yes, I do need your forgiveness. More than that, I don't know what I would have done without you these past weeks. I don't think I could have survived. I really don't."

"Stop, please, you're going to make me cry." Her mouth trembled between a sob and a smile.

"I'd like you to give me another chance. See if I can be the friend you deserve. And the son-in-law."

Abigail reached inside her purse, pulled out a handkerchief, and dabbed at the corners of her eyes. "There. See what you've made me do. Is my makeup a mess?"

"You look fine. As always."

She extracted a compact, examined herself, and closed it with a snap. "I will tell you something I have never told another soul. When my husband and I were first married, he was struggling to set up this company. It was touch and go for a while. He would come home exhausted. More than that. He was terrified of failing."

"He told me of that time," Kenneth said quietly.

"I may not be very religious," Abigail went on determinedly, "but what little I have managed to attain has brought me face-to-face with how I failed him during his hour of greatest need. He needed me to give him strength. He needed me to give him love." Her voice cracked over the words, "And I gave him nothing but demands."

Kenneth waited, marveling that they could be seated there in the same cluttered office where he had once served as her husband's assistant. The woman who had tried with all her might to block his marriage to Kyle, who had treated him from the very first day as an enemy. Yet here they were, talking with an openness that left no room for hiding behind shadows of the past. "I don't think you're a bad person, Abigail."

"Well, I am. I'm a society matron who places far too much importance on what other people think. But there's nothing I can do about the past, and that's not what we're talking about now." She drew herself up by strength of will and continued, "I failed my husband, Kenneth. I do not want to fail my daughter. Or my son-in-law. I have seen how hard it is for a strong man to face defeat. I've learned that the worst suffering is the kind that goes on day in and day out, with no answer and no end in sight."

Kenneth nodded slowly, the power of her understanding almost overwhelming him. "I feel like it's tearing me apart inside."

"I've seen how hard it is for a strong man to turn and look for help. To *ask* for help." Her chin trembled slightly, but she lifted her head and forced herself to remain in control. "I want you to know that I am here to support and encourage you, Kenneth. Day or night. As a friend should be. As family."

She saved him from having to respond immediately by pulling back her cuff to examine her gold watch. "Now we really must be going. If I know my daughter, she will be anxiously watching for us to come."

CHAPTER SIX

"IT'S NOT JUST THE PROBLEMS with the baby," Kenneth confessed as he turned down Connecticut Avenue and joined the heavy morning traffic. "It's everything."

"All the weight of the world has landed on your shoulders," Abigail sympathized.

The gift of being understood opened the door further, freeing him to say what before had escaped words. "Everything's become so confusing, Abigail. On the one hand there's my relationship with God. At this time when He could seem very far away, He is so close to me. Even in the worst moments, I feel His presence. So I pray for baby Charles, I pray for Kyle, I pray for us. But on the other hand, I don't hear anything in reply. Nothing. And that really scares me. How can God be so close and yet so silent?"

"I can't answer you," Abigail sighed. "To be perfectly frank, God has never seemed close to me at all. I'm far too inadequate to offer you anything except a listening ear."

Washington traffic was growing slower every day,

or so it seemed to Kenneth. Especially now, when there was so much pressing him to hurry. More cars, more people, more noise in the urgency of one crisis pushing hard on the feet of the last one. In the past he had made it a point of staying on top of the Washington political scene. Now it was just too difficult. His mind seemed to move at the pace of these overcrowded roads. And every thought was about his wife and his precious little baby.

Kenneth stopped for a traffic light and looked at her. "It's hard to believe we're having this conversation."

Abigail turned her face toward the windshield. Her lovely features tightened and aged. "I have spent a great deal of time watching you since your wedding. I've seen how you are at the company, diligent in your responsibilities and accepting a subordinate position. Anyone else in your place would be demanding a raise and a seat on the board."

"That's simple enough. I've just been so happy with my life, I didn't need to grasp at anything further."

"Wait, let me finish." Abigail continued her inspection of the outside world as Kenneth pulled through the crossroads. "I have also seen you with my daughter. And I have seen you in your worship. You are a good man, Kenneth. You deserve far more than I have been willing to give." Abigail sighed and smiled weakly. "I suppose what I am trying to say is that you are not the only one who needs to apologize."

They drove on in companionable silence as Kenneth entered the tree-lined streets of Georgetown. The car drummed over the rounded cobblestones, passing one quiet residential street after another. Kenneth finally said,

"Do you think this doctor will really have anything new to offer us?"

Abigail hesitated as they turned down Kenneth's street. As soon as their house came into view, the door sprang open and Kyle rushed down the stairs, her impatience evident. Abigail said quietly, "To be frank, I am beginning to feel like anything at all would be better for my daughter than more of this uncertainty."

In the hospital ward, Kenneth stepped back so that he could watch his wife watch the baby. Kyle's face was so drawn she looked older than her mother. It was no longer possible to fool himself. Abigail was right. This uncertainty was killing her.

"Mr. Adams? I'm Dr. Hearly." The beefy man was tall and solid and carried with him an air of confidence. He turned to Abigail. "You must be Mrs. Rothmore."

"I can't thank you enough for seeing us, doctor."

"Yes, well, your friends made quite a case on your behalf." He glanced toward the glass-fronted hospital bassinet. "And now that I have seen the baby, I can well understand why."

He stepped forward to where Kyle stood by the crib, her fingers curled around the top corner of the glass cover. He inspected her face for a moment, his eyes and voice gentling. "And you must be Mrs. Adams."

"He just opened his eyes and looked at me. He can see me through the glass, can't he?" Kyle flashed a frantic glance toward the doctor, then turned back to the crib. "He's getting better. I *know* it."

But the baby did not look well to Kenneth. Not at all.

His own heart ached as he watched the helpless little infant trapped there on the other side of the glass.

The baby's entire body was a faint blue. The eyes were clenched so tight his whole face was twisted and furrowed. Every once in a while the body gave a convulsive shiver, then went still. The little mouth was opened up wide, as though baby Charles wanted to scream and cry. Only there was no noise coming from the crib. None at all.

Kyle's fingers seemed ready to claw through the glass. "Can I hold him?" were the words from her lips, but it was the desperation in her tone and expression that tore at Kenneth's heart.

The doctor continued his careful inspection of Kyle for a moment longer, then turned to the nurse hovering on the bassinet's other side. "Let Mrs. Adams have the baby."

"But, doctor—"

"Give her the baby, nurse." He waited until the nurse had turned off the oxygen and begun unfastening the catches before turning to Kenneth and Abigail. In a low voice he said, "Why don't you both join me in the conference room."

Kenneth turned to his wife. "We won't be long, honey."

But Kyle did not reply. Kenneth wondered if she had even heard him. Her whole being was reaching out along with her arms to accept the tiny bundle.

The doctor waved them into chairs on the table's opposite side. Two thick folders lay open before his own place, along with a pair of empty coffee cups. He glanced at his watch, then at the closed door, and gave a sigh.

Dr. Hearly's gaze was dark and probing. Kenneth sensed he was a man with both intelligence and integrity. This was confirmed to Kenneth when he said, "Long ago I designed a lecture for distraught parents. Most doctors come up with something or other to handle such situations. But I am reluctant to give it here. You both strike me as astute, able to accept the truth."

"The uncertainty—the waiting—has nearly done us all in," Kenneth replied. "I simply can't understand why it has taken so long for the doctors to decide what the matter is."

"They know what the matter is," Dr. Hearly replied. His voice was deep, strong, and had the characteristic of being both direct and gentle at the same time. "The only question is how much hope they can offer you."

Again he glanced at his watch and shook his head. "Excuse me." He reached for the phone and dialed a number. His fingers seemed almost too large for the holes. "This is Dr. Hearly up in Conference Room . . . I'm sorry, I don't know what number . . . oh, you do. Good. Listen, I've been waiting for Dr. Pearce and the pediatric surgeon . . . wait, I have his name here." He inspected the open file. "Yes. Saunders, that's right." He listened a moment, shook his head a second time, and said, "No, that's all right. Thank you for checking."

He placed the receiver back in its cradle and went on. "It seems that Dr. Saunders had to perform an emergency operation and Dr. Pearce is delivering a baby at another hospital. I would have preferred for at least one of them to be present. But I have a conference to get to, and I'm afraid I really can't wait much longer."

"We understand." Abigail glanced at Kenneth to make sure it was all right for her to speak. "You're the expert in this field."

"We'd really like to have your opinion," Kenneth agreed. "Your unvarnished conclusion."

The man gave each of them another swift inspection, then nodded once. "Very well. Mr. Adams, I am sorry to tell you that your son has what we call a shunting across his heart."

My son. The words were enough to stab him deeply. While Kyle was pregnant he often had dreamed of hearing those words. He had never mentioned it—one of the few secrets he had ever kept from her. He had not wanted to say it and then have her feel disappointment for him if the child turned out to be a girl. He knew he would have been delighted with a daughter. But in his heart of hearts he had yearned for a son. Yet now when he heard those longed-for words, they threatened to tear his world apart.

When he was unable to respond, Abigail said for them both, "I'm afraid I don't understand what you mean."

The doctor thumbed through pages in the first file. "I understand from your wife's history that her brother suffers from a heart condition."

"Yes," Kenneth managed. "But her parents are both in excellent health."

"I don't suppose you know her grandparents' medical histories?"

Kenneth started to rise. "No, but I could call and—"

"Later. See to that later and inform Dr. Saunders if

any of them suffered from a heart problem." He closed the file. "Infant cardiology represents an entirely new field. But we are beginning to wonder if there is a genetic basis to some of these ailments."

Abigail reached across the void that seemed to be gathering around Kenneth and took his hand.

"Blood is meant to flow through the heart's valves, you see, moving from one chamber to the next in very careful steps. First blood travels from the heart to the lungs, where it gathers oxygen. Then it returns to the heart and is sent out to the body, carrying oxygen and nourishment." He paused a moment, gathering himself. "At least, that is how it should work. In your son's case, there is a hole. A very large one, I'm sorry to say, which means that the blood is bypassing the system of valves and chambers."

Kenneth felt the void grow and expand until he was lost in the darkness. Helpless and terrified. He clutched at Abigail's hand, yet did not even feel her reach across and place a second hand upon his. He wanted to shout at the doctor, tell him to stop. As if halting the words would make it all untrue. But he could not open his mouth. He was imprisoned. Lost.

"This defect in your son's heart, this hole, means his body is forced to work impossibly hard. Rather than correctly sending the blood into the lungs for nourishment, oxygen-starved blood is being shunted back into his oxygen-starved body. The blueness—you must have noticed the bluish tint to his skin."

"We've noticed," Abigail said, her voice barely a whisper.

"This is caused by a lack of oxygen." He sighed again, flipping through pages to a second file. "Your son is showing all the classic symptoms, I'm afraid. He won't feed and takes all his nourishment from the drip. He has difficulty drawing breath, so we are keeping him on straight oxygen. And there seems to be some fluid buildup in his lungs."

Abigail demanded, "Can't you operate—repair the hole?"

"Not yet." His eyes took on a distant, professorial look. "Some very good work is being done down in Dallas by a certain Dr. Yacoub. But they have never treated someone so young, or someone so seriously affected as your son, I'm afraid. The problem is not the surgical technique but the anesthesia. The risk to newborns is extremely high. We need a new, gentler anesthetic in order to start working with these very young children."

Kenneth clung desperately to the hope enclosed within the first two words. *Not yet.* "How long will we have to wait?"

The dark eyes lifted to Kenneth's and gave him another deep inspection. "If your baby were to survive another ninety days, I would say that it would be worth contacting Dallas."

There he stopped. The silence hung so heavy that Kenneth felt his own lungs were being robbed of air. Finally he managed, "What are you saying?"

Dr. Hearly leaned across the table, closing the space between them. "Mr. Adams, your son's heart is working impossibly hard. A newborn baby simply cannot cope with this strain."

He waited through another long moment, then continued. "It is so hard to know what is correct for a situation like this. But I can see what you must be going through right now, and your wife . . ." He paused and looked at the files as if searching for the next words. "I heard what Dr. Pearce and Dr. Saunders think about the situation before I did my own examination. That is why I decided to speak with you as I have.

"Mr. Adams, all three of us believe your baby's life is unsustainable."

"No," Kenneth moaned. "It can't be. . . ."

"We are doing everything in our power to keep your baby alive," the doctor continued. His voice had the soft, deep rumble of a coming storm. "But his shunt is so large, this defect to his heart so severe, that your baby is not able to help us win."

Abigail recovered enough to whisper, "How long?"

Dr. Hearly's gaze did not waver from Kenneth's face. "You must prepare your wife for the worst, Mr. Adams. Do so without delay."

CHAPTER SEVEN

JOEL WAS AS HAPPY AS he had been in months.

He had always loved trains. As a boy, he watched them thunder by and yearned for faraway places. Now he loved being able to sit back and watch from inside as the world whipped away beyond the window.

He felt Ruthie squeeze his hand and looked into his beloved wife's face. She had returned to her traditional Mennonite dress for their visit home to the farm, putting aside the denim skirt and simple blouses she wore around the mission. Joel had repeatedly told her that she was welcome to wear her Mennonite bonnet and attire, but she explained it could alienate some of the young people who drifted into their mission hall. He had finally stopped bringing up the subject, recognizing the truth in her observation.

But he was very glad to see Ruthie now back in the dress of her heritage. He loved her for who she was, and he loved the family and the tradition which had shaped her. Now that she did not wear Mennonite clothing all the time, seeing her in it brought back many wonderful memories.

Joel's own childhood with Martha and Harry had not been happy. His father had been critically injured in the war and given up for dead. His mother, faced with raising a child alone and without support, had chosen to give up her newborn girl for adoption. Then when his father had finally come home, the joy of their reunion had been darkened by the loss of their daughter. The wounds left on their spirits refused to heal. Joel had been born and raised in a house filled with silent shadows of a past he did not understand. It was the Miller family's arrival in the neighborhood that had begun the transformation, introducing Joel to both a happy family and, eventually, helping to unite his own family in faith.

"You look so happy," Ruthie said, sharing a smile. Her dress now included the starched little cap of a married matron instead of the maiden's scarf.

"I am." He hesitated, not wanting to taint the day but needing to share it all with her. "But I'm also feeling guilty."

"It's only natural." She reached over and laced her other hand into his. "Still, it is not wrong for us to be happy, even when Kyle and Kenneth are suffering."

Joel glanced back out the window, feeling all the conflicting emotions fading with the distance. Not even the very difficult telephone conversation he had with his sister before leaving for the station could keep up with him and the quietly rattling train. "I don't know how we're going to tell them our own news."

She did not ask what he was speaking about. Instead, she lifted his hand with both of hers and held it firmly to her middle. "We will just let God show us the way, my Joel."

A couple passing down the train's central aisle stared at Ruthie in her homespun black dress and long-sleeved blouse and sturdy shoes and little white cap. Joel pulled Ruth's hands back to the central armrest and wished he had his wife's ability to ignore the stares of strangers. "You're losing your accent. You don't say Choel anymore," he commented with a teasing smile.

She laughed. "Give me three minutes with my family, and you will have all the accent you ever want to hear."

Upon their arrival at Lansdale, Pennsylvania, Joel was glad Simon was there to greet them. He was feeling very weary and weak. He tried to hide it from everyone, but he knew Ruthie had noticed what he himself had seen in the train station's mirror—his tightened features, the furrows across his forehead, the sunken eyes. He knew too that his lips were compressing with the effort of holding back the pain in his chest.

Simon embraced his brother-in-law, gave him one long look, and declared, "To home a taxi we must take."

"Simon, no, it is too much." Ruthie looked genuinely alarmed. Farm income had steadily declined over the previous few years, and finances around the Miller household were extremely tight. They were being forced to draw from savings just to put food on the table. "We do not have—"

"It is not too much, and I will pay," Simon announced proudly.

"With what?"

"I will explain soon, sister. But say nothing of this to Papa. Not yet. It is not yet the time for talking of this secret." He gave her a mysterious grin as he hefted Joel's suitcase.

Ruthie glanced at her husband, then decided to accept.

"Let us go, my husband. We can talk of new mysteries when you are rested."

Joel found himself too tired from the journey to resist. The thought of having to wait for a bus, sit through the jouncing series of starts and stops, then walk the long drive up to the farm seemed impossible just then. He said to Simon, "Your accent is stronger since the last time I saw you."

"Yah, hear it every day more myself, I do." He led them over to the Lansdale taxi rank. The driver was a grizzled old man who had long since become accustomed to Mennonite dress. In fact, his only lingering glance was cast at Joel. Simon told the man, "Please can you take us down the Highway Fourteen to where the road ends?"

"Down past the church," the man confirmed, waiting until the three of them had climbed inside. He ground the gears. "Know just where you mean."

Joel sank gratefully into the ancient padding, leaned his head against the window, and closed his eyes. He listened as brother and sister began chatting away in Old German, the soft voices melding and drifting and finally carrying him away into dreams.

Joel awoke to the rare sounds of birdsong. It was so different from the traffic noise that filled every room in their tiny apartment above the mission. He lay in the bed and tried to remember how he had gotten there. A vague memory surfaced of being roused from his sleep in the back of the taxi, and people whispering hellos and guiding him up the stairs and into bed, everybody making a game of his inability to respond.

He rolled over in bed and saw he was alone. A glance out the window told him it was the hour before dawn. The sky was palest blue with hints of coming gold, a farmyard sunrise. He heard a rooster crow and the cows give their lowing call to be milked. A bucket rattled as someone walked whistling across the yard below his window. Joel rolled from his bed and reached for his clothes.

When he appeared on the porch, Mr. Miller was seated in the high-backed chair Joel had made for him the previous summer. The big man's beard was graying fast, and the stump of his leg was propped on a padded stool. The only time he used the stool was when the leg was feeling poorly. Which was more and more often these days.

Mr. Miller's diabetes had brought his family from their farm to the Washington area, and thus into Joel's life, in order to receive treatment for his ailment. It was this illness that had cost him the lower half of his left leg. After the Millers returned to Lansdale, he had thrown himself back into farm work, bravely enduring the awkwardness and pain of a prosthesis. Only in the past year, however, had he finally accepted the family's insistence that he slow down. He refused to discuss his health or even say how he was feeling. But in the early morning light, Joel could see the weary lines etched like ever-deepening furrows that spread out from his eyes and mouth.

But the smile was still fresh and from the heart, and the eyes twinkled in welcome. "So, Choel, you have slept away the trip, yah?" He watched his son-in-law pull over a chair and demanded, "How is the heart?"

"About the same."

"A doctor you have seen?"

"Last week." There was no space for masking news. Not with this good, simple man. "He says he can't explain how I've lasted as long as I have." Joel waved as Simon came around the side of the barn, carrying two full pails. Already the pigs anticipated Simon's arrival and had set up a high-pitched squeal. "Joseph, how is the farm?"

"The farm is in God's hands," the big man replied firmly.

"In his last letter, Simon mentioned possibly selling some land."

"Simon is a good boy. But he clings to his worries. The land, it is my family's for five generations. We do not sell. God, He will show us a way." Joseph Miller studied his work-worn hands before asking, "And your sister Kyle, she has news of her own?"

"They saw another specialist. Kenneth didn't tell me much, only that the news wasn't good."

Joseph Miller nodded slowly, his eyes both bright and troubled. "Hard it is to see young ones suffer, as both of you are, I have asked God, take the burden from you, and give it to me, why not? A good life have I had. The years ahead I would give to you if I could."

Joel felt a lump grow in his throat at all the words contained. "Thank you, Joseph."

"I remember another porch, another time." He looked fondly at his companion. "I remember a young boy who came and prayed with me. I remember thinking, yah, here is one with a heart the angels love."

Joel watched his wife scurry across the yard, cradling newly gathered eggs in her apron. As she climbed the stairs she gave them a from-the-heart smile before entering the house.

"I remember how this young man said no to a woman who loved him," Joseph continued quietly. "Not because he did not love her. No. Because he loved her too much. I remember how he tried to keep his pain and his future to himself. I remember how he gave his days to his Lord.

Yah, all this do I remember, that and more." The long gray beard slowly rose and fell. "Right there before my eyes, I saw a wonder. Yah, a miracle. I saw the Lord at work in a man."

Joel looked at the older man and saw the wisdom in his eyes. "I'm scared of the future, Joseph. Terrified."

"Yah, hard it is to face what we know is coming." He gave a gentle emphasis to the word *we*. "And know I do what you wish to hear. You say with your eyes, 'Tell me all will be fine. Tell me I will grow to see sons of my own. Tell me this wonderful wife, we will share many years together.' "

A breath of morning wind skirted the house and found them there on the corner of the porch. It ruffled Joseph's beard, making it seem as though the man was laughing silently. Or crying. Or both.

"Choel, I love you as my own. If I could give you all the years left, I would do it. Right here and now." He held out two scarred, strong hands. "But the Lord, He has not given me this power. So only can I tell you, trust in Him. Remember the goal, my friend. Offer this is all I can for you now."

"Tell me again." He swallowed with difficulty. "I forget sometimes."

"Ah, now you choke with old Choseph. Forget that you never will. The Lord, He has written it upon your heart." The kindly eyes inspected him. "No, the forgetful mind, it comes with age. You can help me remember, yah?"

He managed a little smile. "Maybe so."

"Very well, then." Joseph leaned forward until the tip of his beard brushed against the leg propped on the stool. "When we stand before the Lord—help me here. What is it we hope and pray to hear?"

Joel whispered, " 'Well done, thou good and faithful servant.' "

"Ach, yah. That it is." He leaned farther still, closing the distance between them, until his gaze filled Joel's vision, and all Joel could hear were the softly murmured words, "Well done."

CHAPTER EIGHT

KYLE SAT IN THE DOCTOR'S outer office, blindly turning pages of a magazine. Her mind was unable to focus on the words, but it gave her hands something to do. She kept her face turned downward so she did not need to look at the others in the waiting room, especially the woman with her two children on the other side. One of the children was crying fretfully, and the sound grated on Kyle's nerves until she felt ready to scream.

She found herself recalling her conversation with Joel that morning. Her brother had called to say they were going up to the Miller farm for a few days, something about wanting to help out in some way with all the problems the Millers were facing. Or perhaps it was something else, and she had been unable to concentrate enough to understand. Then Joel had said, "We miss seeing you around the mission, Kyle."

For some reason, her mind had fastened on that. As it had the evening before, when Kenneth had told her she needed to get out, do something beyond her visits to the hospital. "Have you talked with my husband?"

The question and its tone clearly unsettled him. "Well,

yes, we talked earlier this—"

"I can't believe this. It's like a conspiracy." She heard the cold sharpness invade her voice. Part of her said it was uncalled for, but even so it gave her a sense of satisfaction to speak like this. "Why are you trying to pull me away from my baby's side?"

"Kyle, nobody is trying to do anything like—"

"Well, I won't do it, I'm telling you." Her voice rose an octave. "My baby needs me. I'm doing everything I can, even if no one else will."

"We all are," Joel said calmly, and Kyle recognized the tone he used with the toughest and angriest of the young people who entered his mission. "We are praying every day for your baby's health. And yours. And Kenneth's."

She wanted to shout at him that Kenneth did not need the prayers, that neither did she, that everything was needed for her baby. But she could not say the words. "I know where I am supposed to be."

And then it had hit her. A thought so sudden and powerful that now as she sat in the doctor's office she could not even recall how her conversation with Joel had ended. The thought had locked into her mind, making her wonder why it had not come to her before. Kyle had called the doctor's office and *demanded* an appointment that very morning.

"Mrs. Adams? Kyle?" The receptionist gave her a warmly sympathetic smile. Everyone in Dr. Pearce's office knew what she was going through. "Dr. Pearce will see you now. You know where his office is, don't you, dear?"

She hurried down the long hallway and entered the open doorway. The old doctor was bent over his desk, writing on a form. He looked up at the sound of her footsteps and gave his patented weary smile. "Kyle, how are you, my dear?"

"I'm angry, that's how I am." She seated herself and

rested her purse on her knees, gripping the clasp with both hands. "I want to know why you never warned me this could happen."

He studied her a moment, his brow furrowed. Then he closed the file before him and leaned back in his chair. "I'm not sure I understand."

"I'm talking about my brother Joel's heart. You knew all along there was the risk that my baby would be born sick like him. Why didn't you warn me?"

"Kyle, my dear . . ." Dr. Pearce closed his eyes and pinched the bridge of his nose. "Has Kenneth spoken to you?"

"About what?" She could hear the same shrill tone returning that had emerged in her conversation with Joel. "He started on about something last night, but I stopped him. Just like I'm stopping you. This is a conspiracy, isn't it? I can tell. Everybody's talking behind my back. Well, I want it stopped, do you hear me? Stopped right now!"

Dr. Pearce observed her with grave concern. When she had stopped and was breathing heavily, he said, "Kyle, you have to stop thinking this way. It is the grief talking, not you."

"Why should I feel grief? My baby is going to be fine!"

He did not even acknowledge that she had spoken. "In the first place, there was no way we could have predicted that your baby would be born with an impaired heart."

"But Joel—"

"Yes, Joel has a heart condition. But yours is fine, Kyle. And so are the hearts of both your birth parents. We have also asked them about their families, and so far as they know there has been no previous record of heart problems." He studied her face. "So you see, my dear, there was no way anyone could have predicted this."

"There must have been. You missed something, or they

didn't tell you everything." Her hands gripped the purse tighter.

"Kyle," he said, drawing the word out into a long sigh. "I don't normally do this, but I am going to prescribe something for you. I want you to take one of these tablets every morning and evening. Will you do that for me?"

Kyle waited while he scribbled on the little white pad; then she accepted the slip of paper and walked out. As she left the office she decided she would go directly to the hospital. It did not matter what anyone said. Charles was there and Charles needed her. She would sit there and let him know that someone loved him and wanted him to get better. He was going to get better.

Kyle's limbs felt leadened as she left the hospital. Had they let her, she would have stayed on. She hated to leave. There really was no reason for going home anyway. Her baby remained there in the stark, antiseptic hospital ward. That was where she belonged as well.

She had stood there for hours, looking down at her baby. He remained shut off from her by the protective incubator glass. Each rise and fall of the tiny chest had made her wish to gasp in response, as though she might breathe on his behalf. Her arms ached to hold him. To draw him close to her bosom and provide the nourishment that would sustain the little life. To cuddle him close and whisper in his ear the words of endearment that only a mother knows. To feel the beat of the small heart and the warmth of his body cradled against her.

But the entire time she had stood there, the glass partition had mocked her feelings. Her arms had remained empty—empty and yet at the same time heavy. She could only wait and pray and plead with whispered messages through the glass for the baby not to give up. Beg her child to fight on, strive to take another breath, and for the little damaged heart to continue to beat. *Please. Beat again.*

Kyle had laid her head on her arms and rested on the cold glass surface. The pleas came from her very soul. She was so helpless. So removed. So shut away from the infant that was hers. Over and over she silently shouted a single thought, one which rang through her heart's empty recesses, *This isn't how it is meant to be.*

Now as Kyle walked away from the hospital, she heard the nurse's insistent tones drone through her head. "It's time for you to leave for the day, Mrs. Adams." As if anyone had the right to tear her away from her baby. But the nurse had spoken with such authority and finality that Kyle had not dared to argue.

But as she walked she felt resentment building inside of her. What right did they have to treat her as though she had no authority over the care of her own child? *She* should be the one to demand, "It's time for you to leave for the day, nurse." Why couldn't she have her own baby in her own home like a normal mother? Why the daily trips to the hospital ward to peer anxiously through a glassed partition, her fingers numb with the ache to caress, her ears straining to hear each breath, her whole body tensing at each small movement. Why?

Kyle knew the answer—it was the tiny defective heart. But why, with all of their knowledge and all of their fancy equipment, why couldn't they *do* something? Kyle often found herself wanting to scream, *Do something now!*

But Kyle did not express the cry of her heart. They had to be patient, Kenneth often reminded her. They had to pray, and to trust. But Kyle wondered how much longer she could hold on. Her faith seemed to be slipping from her just as surely as her frail baby. It was frightening. She did not want to lose her grip on God any more than she wished to lose the fragile hold on her weakening child.

"If only . . ." The anguish filling her heart pushed her harder than the brisk wind as she walked toward the bus stop. "If only I hadn't insisted on finding my birth parents. If I could have just let things be as they were. If I hadn't discovered a brother with a heart problem, everything might be all right. Why wasn't I content simply to be a Rothmore? Why. . . ?"

A part of her knew the recriminations were foolish. Even as she raged inwardly, trapped and hurting and wanting desperately to be with her child, even now she knew the words made no sense. But Kyle's tired and troubled mind was beyond reason. She ached. She mourned. She fought against reality. She sought explanations that would not come. She clung to hopes that did not exist, not even in her own mind. She fought a losing battle with her own exhausted resources. It was all she had left.

CHAPTER NINE

THE MORNING BREAKFAST DISHES had been cleared away, the old table scrubbed clean, and the family was seated and watching Joel. Joel in turn was watching Simon, the high school friend who had brought him into this wonderful family. Simon, the eldest boy, was Joel's age, and farm work had chiseled strength into his young features.

Joel then glanced at Sarah, Ruthie's younger sister. She was entering her middle teens and growing into a person of beauty, the kind that shines from within. She had her mother's poise and her father's eyes, a gaze so level and direct that most young men even twice her age found themselves stammering and blushing.

Joseph Miller cleared his throat. "No harder can the family be listening than now, Choel."

Joel felt hesitant and shy and eager, all at once. "I don't know where to start."

"But start you must, or make the explosion, and think of the mess that would make in Mama's kitchen."

His wife chided, "Papa, shah, what a thing to say."

Joel looked at Ruthie and implored, "You tell them."

"But you said you wanted to be the one."

"I can't. You do it."

"What?" Joseph cried. "Also Ruthie is having news? Too much this is for one old heart. One of the two must wait until another day."

"Papa." This time his wife's warning tone was genuine. "Now are you stopping with the chokes?"

Joel sat surrounded by the love of family. It was so good to be able to smile again. To feel the moment's joy well up until his weak heart felt ready to take wings and fly from his chest. When his wife looked his way again, he nodded and said, "Go ahead, Ruthie—tell them."

Ruthie took a breath that seemed to go on forever, then she announced, "We are going to have a baby."

"A grandpa!" Joseph fairly shouted the words. "You are to be making of me a grandpa!"

Mother and daughter were already up and moving toward each other. They stood by the table and hugged fiercely while all the others shouted and cheered the news. Joel accepted the handshakes and the backslaps and thought he could never be happier than this moment. Not even his wedding day had compared with this overflowing of shared joy, of shared future.

For the rest of that morning and throughout the afternoon, the entire farm was electric with laughter and chatter about names, about boys versus girls, about family legacies. Joel found enough strength so that he could walk with Simon through the day's work. That afternoon, Simon invited him to go along to the Brueder farm. Simon had been calling on the middle daughter, a lovely young woman named Patience. She carried her name with grace, a quiet, steady girl who reminded Joel of Simon's mother. She had been Ruthie's friend all their lives, and her joy over Joel's news was something to behold.

The Brueders made them both welcome with buoyant noise, full of jokes and plannings and heavily accented English. The two men returned home with the sunset, the horse-drawn cart full of boisterous laughter and shared memories.

But when they pulled into the Miller farm, they were greeted with silence and lengthening shadows. Even the farm animals seemed subdued. Simon exchanged a puzzled glance with Joel, then frowned, and instantly Joel knew Simon feared for his father.

They leaped from the cart and raced up the stairs and through the front door. Relieved to see Joseph seated at the table, they were slowed by the sound of quiet weeping.

Joel looked from one tearstained face to the other before saying, "It's Charles Kenneth, isn't it?"

"Yah, yah," Joseph Miller sadly rumbled. "The little baby, he has gone home."

CHAPTER TEN

THE SUMMER HEAT HUNG as heavy as the clouds, thick and cloying. The day begged for rain, but none fell. The air was still and hot and hard to breathe. The somber group that had gathered for Charles Kenneth's funeral took their cues from the day.

Kyle sat in the church's front row. Kenneth was there beside her, weeping softly. Abigail was on her other side, alternating between stubborn stoicism and heaving sobs. Beside her sat Martha and Harry Grimes, both of them far beyond the power of speech. Throughout the service, Kyle remained so quiet and still her black veil did not even move with her breath. She had no more tears to weep.

She had shed the last tear back in the hospital, when she had appeared in time to see the frantic activity surrounding her baby's crib. So many people had gathered and reached in and pulled over equipment and prepared syringes and shouted in panic-stricken voices that she could not even see her child.

Her scream was so loud it had felt as though her throat had split. Her cry had shocked the entire tableau into stillness. Two of the nurses had hurried forward to catch and hold her away from the crib. But the young doctor had been there and called to them in a sharp voice of his own.

They had formed an aisle of mourners, those doctors and nurses. She flew through them and collapsed there before the small bed. She threw her arms around the tiny baby boy and emptied her heart of everything that was left. All feeling, all hope, all life of her own. All had flowed out to spill upon the baby she had lost.

After the church service, Kyle felt a moment's overwhelming anguish when the people rose to watch them leave. It came and went too quickly for her to speak, even if she had had the strength to utter a word. Then she slipped back into the shell that had enveloped her ever since leaving the hospital that day. She was glad for this shell. It was her preservation. It kept her from going insane—not from grief, but from emptiness. The rebellion passed, and Kyle managed to stand on her own strength. She felt Kenneth grasp one arm and Abigail the other. Together they turned and followed the tiny coffin, borne in the arms of one pallbearer, down the aisle and out of the church.

The drive to the cemetery took forever, yet was over in minutes. Kyle allowed hands to guide her into a chair at the side of the grave. The void at the center of her being filtered everything. The moment lacked color. It was as gray and featureless as the sky. Still, she managed to hear the weeping which surrounded her. Across the grave from where she sat, the Miller family stood and keened with grief. Numbly she wondered why they should cry now. Charles Kenneth was gone. It was too late to cry. Too late to hope, to pray, to beg for help of any kind. Nothing mattered anymore.

One conviction surfaced during the time she sat there at the graveside. Just as the pastor stopped speaking and the impossible moment loomed as great and dark as the mouth of the grave, Kyle thought, *It should be me*. Her baby should be alive. She should be the one they lowered into the earth. For though she was living and seated between Kenneth and Abigail, still she was going down into the grave with her child. Her life was totally meaningless.

CHAPTER ELEVEN

"MISS KYLE, I BELIEVE YOU promised that charity shop over on Seventh Street some clothes or somethin'."

Kyle raised her head to look at the young woman who spoke through the open door. Abigail had promptly sent one of her maids over soon after the funeral, and she had been with them since. But for the life of her Kyle could not remember the young woman's name, despite the fact that Kyle had previously seen her at Abigail's any number of times. Kyle fleetingly wished it could be Maggie standing there, the housekeeper from her childhood and a treasured friend. But Maggie was ill, so sick she had not even been able to travel for the baby's funeral.

Kyle looked back down at the Bible in her lap. She had been attempting to read a Scripture portion, or at least she had been going through the motions. She could not remember a single word from the passage. Certainly nothing had touched her heart. How could it when her heart felt like a rock in the middle of her chest?

"Miss Kyle?"

She looked up again and nodded her head. The charity on Seventh Street? Yes, she vaguely remembered their call.

It had been back in her previous life when she was rushing to get to the hospital. It seemed like an eternity ago. Everything did, before that last day. . . .

When Kyle made no effort to stir from her chair, the maid said that someone was waiting downstairs and asked Kyle what she would like her to do.

Kyle laid aside her Bible and rose to her feet. The exertion cost her a deep, weary sigh. Even living and breathing was a heavy strain.

"Tell them I'll be right down," she instructed. She brushed listless hands over the dark skirt that seemed a reflection of her feelings.

The maid turned and was gone. Kyle could hear the brisk footsteps echo through the hall. Kyle found such purposefulness, such liveliness, irritating and out of place. And at the same time she knew her attitude was unreasonable and also out of place.

She sighed again and turned to the door.

Where did I put those clothes I gathered? Kyle wondered vaguely as she left her room and started down the hall. For a moment she could not even remember what lay behind the other doors of her own upstairs. She pressed a hand to her forehead, trying to concentrate. Her room? No. She had wanted the things out of her closet so she had room to sort out and put away garments prone to picking up lint from the baby's blankets. *Her baby.* The unbidden thought rocked Kyle. She stopped in midstep, then forced herself onward.

The closet in their guest bedroom. She remembered now. She had placed them on the shelf in the large closet. . . .

Kyle pushed open the door before her, and momentum carried her into the room.

But it was not the guest room. In her confusion she had

opened the door to the nursery.

The room was just as she had last seen it, the day of her last visit to the hospital, the day she last . . . She took in the entire room in a single glance. The baby bed, hung with soft draping tapestries. The blue-and-white teddy there beside the pillow, waiting patiently with its big soulful eyes. The chest of drawers, its top arrayed with baby bath needs, including a pile of tiny diapers. A pair of bottles on the windowsill caught the light and reflected it into the room.

Kyle stepped back, her shoulder bumping hard into the solid oak doorframe as she pushed her way out of the room. She frantically fumbled about, reaching with numb fingers and finally gripping the door handle, then slamming it with both hands. The noise echoed up and down the hallway.

From behind the closed door came the tinkling music of the small merry-go-round on the baby's bedside table.

Kyle lurched back down the hall, her hands curled into tight fists. She had not meant to enter that room. She was not sure if she would ever be able to. She certainly could not face it yet.

She stopped and gripped the banister at the top of the stairs, fighting for control. Her baby was gone. There was nothing to be done about it. She would not think about it. She would not cry anymore. She would push all thoughts and all feelings far down, away from her aching, empty heart.

Slowly her shoulders straightened. She took a steadier breath. Yes. That was the answer. It was the *only* solution. She would keep all of it locked down tight. She would not let any of it out. Not ever again.

The solid wood banister felt cold and hard under her grip. She found security in its solidity.

The charity. They were waiting downstairs. The sound

of voices from the hall below gave her the courage to straighten her skirt and walk to the correct bedroom.

As she gathered the items hurriedly into her arms, her resolve strengthened. She must guard herself. She must by force of will preserve this facade and never permit anything to shatter it again.

With a lifted chin and a steady gait, she began her descent of the stairs with the bundle of clothes. She would tell them to return for another donation the following week. The maid could prepare everything in the nursery. Yes. And she could go for a long walk until everything was gone.

When Kenneth opened their front door, Joel's first thought was how the man had aged. Looking at his face, it would be easier to believe years had passed, and not just weeks since the baby's funeral.

Kenneth worked the muscles of his face into the semblance of a smile. "Hello, everyone," he said to the group on their doorstep.

Martha brushed by Joel, arms outstretched. "How are you, dear?" Her genuine care and concern gave the common greeting deep meaning.

"Surviving." He closed his eyes as she held him close, and Joel reflected that he had never seen a man look so weary. "Taking it one day at a time."

"Not much else you can do," Harry said, reaching forward to grip Kenneth's arm. "We're right here for you, son."

"Thanks, Harry." But the voice sounded empty. He turned and gave Ruthie a hug, shook Joel's hand, then motioned everyone inside. He shut the door behind them and called, "Honey, look who's here."

Kyle's appearance at the top of the stairs shocked them all to silence. She descended and entered the front hallway without any effort to greet them. Her eyes, cold and utterly blank, made no contact with any of them. Joel searched for words he could offer that might bridge the barriers around his sister.

Finally Martha forced her way forward and reached out her arms. Kyle's stiff shoulders and unresponsive demeanor showed she did not wish to be embraced. So Martha settled hands upon her shoulders and leaned forward. Kyle closed her eyes and held herself absolutely still as Martha kissed her cheek.

Joel watched how Kenneth gazed in deep concern at his wife. The way Kyle endured the greetings from her family clearly pained him. Finally Kenneth said, "Let's go sit down in the living room."

Kyle moved silently in with the others and yet was not there with them. Her face remained blank, her eyes expressionless. Kenneth stood in the doorway and watched as Martha settled down beside her daughter.

"How are you, dear?" Martha asked, her voice low and full of love.

"I'm fine, thank you." The words came out as meaningless sounds. "How are you?"

"We're all very worried about you." Martha's hand reached up to stroke Kyle's hair. There was a flinching move away. Martha's hand fell back to her lap. "Is there anything I can do?"

"Nobody can do anything anymore. It's too late."

Kenneth sighed and shook his head. "Can I get anybody anything?"

Ruthie's stricken look and tear-filled eyes gave Joel the

fleeting impression that she was feeling everything Kyle was not permitting herself to feel. Ruthie silently gazed at Kyle, then her eyes dropped to her folded hands, and Joel knew she was praying.

Harry looked at Kenneth and said, "I'll have a soda if you've got one."

"Sure."

Joel followed Kenneth into the kitchen. "What's happening?"

"You can see for yourself," Kenneth replied wearily. "She's been like this since the funeral. Nothing reaches her. Nothing gets through."

"She must not isolate herself from us," Joel said. "She has to allow herself to grieve."

"That's exactly what the doctor says." Kenneth pried off the bottle top and started back to the living room. "Until she opens up and lets it out, she can't begin to find peace. It wrenches my insides to see her isolating herself even from God."

Joel followed him back down the hall and entered the parlor in time to hear Kyle tell Martha, "I'm coping, Martha. Isn't that what everybody wants me to do? Cope."

"I want you to get better," Martha said, her voice wobbly. Harry accepted the glass from Kenneth, his eyes reflecting his wife's pain. Martha went on, "I want you to recover."

Kyle did not respond for a long moment. When she did speak, it was in a voice that sounded as though it had traveled a thousand miles. "I'm not the one who needed to recover. The battle is over now. It doesn't matter anymore. Nothing does."

Ruthie looked up, the tears filling her eyes and spilling over. She gave Joel a pleading look. He stepped over to where he could look into Kyle's face. "We miss you down at the mission, sister."

She raised her head, and for an instant something flickered deep within her gaze. It came and went so swiftly that Joel could not be certain what it was he had seen. A cold rage? Perhaps. Whatever it was, it left his heart thumping painfully.

Kyle dropped her gaze to the floor at her feet. Her voice remained flat, empty. "What good would I do there? I'd just be in the way."

"That's not true," Ruthie pleaded softly. "Please, Kyle, come down and keep me company. I miss you so."

To this Kyle did not reply at all. The silence continued until Harry drained his glass, set it down, and rose to his feet, a single motion that was enough to lift the others. He bent down and gave Kyle a one-armed hug, so unexpected that she did not have time to flinch away. "We'll see you soon, honey."

Martha followed his lead, her embrace as fierce as it was fleeting. "Let us know if there's anything at all we can do for you."

Ruthie bent over and hugged her then. Kyle closed her eyes as the embrace continued, but at least she did not pull away. Ruthie rose up, leaving a wet spot on Kyle's cheek where their faces had touched. "You stay in my prayers, Kyle, daily."

Harry patted Kenneth's shoulder as he passed, then left his hand in place, turning Kenneth around and pulling him down the hall and through the door. Joel followed them out into the open air and heard Harry ask, "How are you holding up, Kenneth?"

Kenneth seemed about to fall, held aloft only by Harry's hand and his own grim resolve. "Oh, Harry, I don't know how much more of this I can stand. I've lost both of them."

"Why don't you and I get together and do a little walking," Harry suggested, his tone tinged by shared sorrow. "See if I can't help you share this load."

Joel felt something rise from his chest, closing his throat and burning his eyes. He stood there and remembered those other times, when bitterness and unspoken rage turned the atmosphere in his childhood home acrid and smoky. Now Joel stood and watched his father give Kenneth a one-armed hug, and he felt the Lord reach out through the man. "Yes, I have forgiven him," Joel whispered to the Lord. "And I thank you that you can now love Kenneth through my father."

Joel heard Kenneth murmur, "There's no need to burden you with this, Harry."

"I've got a lifetime's experience dealing with impossible situations and impossible people, especially myself." Harry drew him close a second time. "Give me a call, why don't you? We'll wear out some shoe leather and have ourselves a good talk." When Kenneth did not reply, Harry asked, "Do you have anyone else to talk with?"

That brought out a smile. "You won't believe this, but Abigail and I have had a couple of amazing chats."

Martha descended the stairs to stand beside Joel and say, "Abigail Rothmore?"

"Doesn't surprise me in the slightest," Harry said. "Beneath that frosty exterior the Lord is thawing out a frozen heart."

"Abigail doesn't think she really knows God," Kenneth replied slowly.

Harry gave the morning's first genuine smile. "That may be so—at present. But believe me, God knows Abigail."

Martha moved up and took her husband's free hand, and shook her head. "You should hear yourself talk," she said, her voice warm.

"If the Lord can make a change in me," Harry replied, "He can do it in anyone."

Harry looked up at the silent house, then turned back to Kenneth and said softly, "You just remember that."

CHAPTER TWELVE

KYLE WAS BARELY AWARE of the table in front of her. She merely knew that she and Kenneth were going through the motions of sharing another meal together in their cherry-paneled dining room.

There was stirring about her as dishes were placed on the table. Kenneth thanked the maid and told her she was free to go. He made polite conversation with Kyle, mentioning something about a new movie that had opened downtown called *Dr. Zhivago*. He asked if she would like to go. Kyle's headshake was so small it might have been mistaken for a shiver.

She was not the least bit hungry. She didn't care that today was the maid's last day with them, that tomorrow the young woman was scheduled to return to Abigail's. She had heard Kenneth offer the maid his sincere thanks for all her help during their difficult days, but Kyle could not think of anything to add.

As had become a tradition in their home, Kenneth reached for her hand, and she bowed her head for the saying of grace. The words were little more than a rustle on her inner emptiness. She heard the familiar "Amen" and lifted her head, ready to spread her napkin over her knees.

But Kenneth did not let go. "Your hand is cold."

She gave a little shrug and tried to draw away. His grip tightened slightly.

"I think it would be a good idea for you to see Dr. Pearce," her husband said.

That comment did register. She had no plans to see the doctor ever again. Nor any other doctor, for that matter. The whole medical profession had miserably failed her baby. She gave Kenneth a direct look, then her eyes slid away. "I'm fine." The words had been repeated so often over the past weeks and months that they came and went without conscious thought.

"You look pale."

"I tell you, I'm fine."

"I'm worried, honey. You're not sleeping well."

Kyle wished she had the energy to respond. She had lost her baby two months ago, yet he was fussing over paleness and lack of sleep. What could he possibly expect? But she did not have either the interest or the energy to involve herself in such a discussion.

But Kenneth did not let the matter drop. "If I make an appointment, will you go see him?"

"Why?" Kyle's voice sounded empty even to her own ears.

"Because I'm not certain you're as fine as you keep saying. You're pale. You're losing weight. Your hands are cold. You have no appetite. What more do you need to convince you that—"

"What could a doctor do?"

"Well, at least let him see you, then maybe . . ." He trailed off uncertainly. "Maybe a tonic," he finished lamely.

Kyle tossed her napkin on the table and pushed herself

to her feet. *A tonic is not what I need*, she wanted to scream at him. *My baby is.*

But she did not say the words. Instead she looked coolly down at her husband and spoke in an even, controlled tone. "I have a bit of a headache. If you'll excuse me, I believe I'll take a tablet and lie down."

"Kyle——" Kenneth rose to his feet and started to reach for her, but she turned swiftly away. Her last brief glance at his face caught his deep pain at her rejection, his frustration that he could not help her. But she did not stop. She could not help him any more than she could help herself.

Abigail sat in the foyer of Chez François, eyes nervously scanning the crowds on the sidewalk outside. The chic restaurant was located just off Embassy Row, and the midday diners were the cream of Washington society. She glanced at her watch once more, aware that the maitre d' was watching her. It was only because she was a regular that he had held her table this long.

A couple she knew vaguely entered the restaurant, deep in discussion about a new exhibition at the National Gallery. They halted their conversation long enough to greet her warmly. Just as the maitre d' led them away to their table, her daughter pushed through the tall double doors. Abigail sprang to her feet. "Kyle, you're here!"

Kyle shook the worst of the rain off her coat. "You did invite me."

"Yes, well," Abigail hesitated, then decided not to mention that her daughter was forty-five minutes late for the luncheon appointment, or that Kyle had refused even to confirm whether she would come at all. Only that she would think about it. Abigail watched how she stiffened as the hostess reached to help with her coat, and knew a kiss and a hug would not be welcome. "What with this weather, I was almost unable to get here myself. Come, let's see if they held our reservation."

The restaurant manager was a gentleman of the old school who greeted both lunch and dinner crowds in a white bow tie and tails. He held the oversized luncheon menus like a banner and bowed ceremoniously. "Mrs. Rothmore, how kind of you to join us."

"Hello, Raymond. You remember my daughter, Kyle Adams." Which was a fib, but a small one. Kyle had never come here before, since the society circuit was something Kyle generally avoided.

Another formal bow. "Mrs. Adams, what a pleasure it is to see you again. Now if you ladies will please step this way."

Kyle hesitated at the doorway into the main restaurant. Abigail found herself looking at it through her daughter's eyes—the glitter and the mahogany and all the polished people making Washington chatter and polite laughter. She reached down and grasped her daughter's hand, and felt a flash of guilt for all the times she had done so in the past—how she had done so with impatience and demands and antagonism, dragging the sensitive child hither and yon to fulfill her own selfish ambitions. But there was none of that now, only love and concern and a wishing she could give her daughter strength and calm.

When Kyle gave her fingers a nervous squeeze and started forward, Abigail smiled. Sadly, regretfully, aware of past mistakes. But a smile nonetheless.

Twice Abigail was stopped on the way to her table by people who wanted to say hello. Kyle tried to hold back, but at the second table a very well-connected lady, whose name Abigail could not recall, gushed, "And who is this *lovely* young thing here with you?"

"My daughter," Abigail said, glancing over in time to see Kyle wince as attention turned her way. It had been a mistake, Abigail decided, inviting Kyle here and trying to draw her out. "Kyle Adams."

"Why, Abigail, of course I've heard of your lovely daughter. Kyle, I haven't seen you since you were in crinoline and ribbons. How are you, my dear?"

Abigail was watching closely enough to actually see it happen. The surprise registered on Kyle with a little start and a blink and a flash of awareness. Abigail felt excitement race up her spine as she realized what had just occurred. Kyle had met someone who did not immediately associate her with a baby who was no more. She was talking to someone who did not probe or offer sympathy or cause her new agony.

"Fine," Kyle said tentatively with a nod. "I'm fine."

She did not look fine, Abigail knew. She looked hollow. The baby had been gone only three months now, and her daughter's eyes were encircled by dark shadows. But the woman showed a Washington society lady's ability to ignore anything and everything; she gave another exuberant smile and said, "My dears, you really must let me invite you over for tea sometime."

"We'd love to, wouldn't we, Kyle?" Because this society matron had drawn Kyle out, even momentarily, Abigail gave her a heartfelt smile. Then she turned and said, "Come along, sweetheart. Raymond is waiting."

Kyle seemed to peer out from the depths of her own personal foxhole as Raymond held her chair, tucked the napkin across her lap, then went through the list of the day's specials. Abigail normally shooed the little man away, but seeing Kyle's reaction, she engaged him in conversation, making him linger with remarks about this and that. Always with a warm smile for her daughter, trying to show that here Kyle could be safe and public at the same time. Showering her daughter with attention, pretending there was absolutely nothing to the moment beyond the empty conversation that had filled so much of her life. Only now she was desperate to reach her daughter with something, *anything* that might draw her from the empty darkness there behind her gaze.

And because it seemed to be working, at least a little, when Raymond finally departed Abigail leaned across the table and said with an enthusiasm she herself had not felt since the funeral, "Do you know what we should do after lunch? Go shopping and buy you a lovely new dress."

Kyle's nod seemed to Abigail like an incredible victory.

CHAPTER THIRTEEN

HARRY AND KENNETH HAD TAKEN to walking down by the C&O canal in Georgetown twice a week, threading their way through and around the incredible mixture of people. Young lovers strolled arm in arm, enjoying the soft autumn light and the quiet music of sunsets. Children blew paper boats across the canal's still water, and Kenneth would often stop to watch them. The smile on his face twisted Harry's heart, so he could scarcely talk for a while.

These came to be remarkable times for both of them. They could go for an entire walk without speaking more than a few words. On other occasions they talked so much they would not even notice night's descent. The unspoken need was for honesty above all else—that and the companionship of friends. Harry found himself planning his weeks around these Tuesday and Thursday walks.

This evening it was a mixture of long silences broken by disjointed snatches of talk.

"Joel and Ruthie got back from the Miller farm last night. They went up for the harvest celebration," Harry was saying. "Only it doesn't seem like there was much celebrating going on."

Kenneth still wore his business suit, as he had come straight from the office. It was warm for mid-October, without a trace of autumn in the air. The August heat had hung on stubbornly, turning the weeks into a long extension of summer. "Times are hard?" he asked, loosening his tie and removing his coat.

"And getting tougher all the time." Whatever the subject, Harry loved these walks. It was more than just his growing friendship with Kenneth. Somehow their walks seemed to bring him closer to God. As though he was giving feet and a voice to the Spirit, being there for this good man in his hour of need. "Ruthie says the whole community is going through a bad time. Can hardly get enough for their produce to pay for next year's planting."

"Farm prices are at rock bottom," Kenneth agreed. "Our agricultural division has been seeing a record number of bankruptcies. You tell the Millers if they ever need a hand to let me know."

"I'll do that, but I don't think it'll do much good. They're a funny lot. Don't ever borrow. Never been in debt, far as I know." They walked on together as night gradually dropped its dark blanket into place. "How're your own folks doing?"

"Fine," Kenneth replied, the word more breathed than spoken. "They don't really understand what's going on. My parents are solid New England stock. They keep wanting to tell Kyle to just get on with her life, as though pushing her forward would solve all our problems." He shook his head. "We're not seeing a lot of them right now."

It was Harry's turn to ask, "So how's my little girl?"

"Pretty much the same, Harry." It was standard fare, this question and Kenneth's reply. Never brought out first thing, yet always asked and dealt with swiftly. Only tonight there was a slight addition. "She's talking with Abigail about maybe going to church with her one Sunday."

"Hey, that's something." Harry had to grin. "Who'd have ever thought that it'd be mother taking daughter to church?"

Kenneth smiled briefly but turned serious again. "Church for Abigail has been nine parts society and one part God."

"Don't be too hard on the old girl, now."

"Oh, I know she's doing wonders for Kyle. They get together every other day or so. And Kyle actually talks now. The problem is, Kyle's adopting a lot of her mother's attitudes and actions." Kenneth looked at the older man. "My becoming a friend of Abigail's doesn't mean I'm blind to her faults."

But Harry's mind and heart were snagged by something else. "I didn't know Kyle was getting out so much. Do you think she might give Martha a call so they could get together and do something?"

Kenneth stopped and turned to Harry, his forehead creased in sympathy. Harry pressed on. "Martha's been calling Kyle a couple of times a week. If she manages to get Kyle at all she can't get a word in before the girl runs her excuse of the day up the flagpole and hangs up. It's hard on Martha."

"I can imagine." In the distance a group of long-haired kids circled a girl with a guitar. Her strummings carried clearly in the still air. "Harry, I can't bring that up without causing an argument. And there are too many of those anyway. And even if I did, it wouldn't do any good."

"All she needs——"

"Look." Kenneth sighed and started back down the path. "It seems like you and Martha, well, you make her *feel* too much. Does that make any sense?"

"I'm not sure." Harry had trouble sorting through the

pain in his heart and hearing what his mind was saying. "Maybe."

"Being with Abigail is *safe*. They get together and they go shopping or they have lunch or they go to one of these charity events. Kyle doesn't have to feel much of anything. The conversation can be light and easy—you know how Washington society is."

"No, but I can imagine. A lot of chrome and polish."

"Exactly. Kyle can talk endlessly about nothing more demanding than a new hairstyle or the latest bit of gossip or who's going to invite us over for dinner." He jammed his fists deep into his pockets. "That's our conversation these days at home. If I try to bring up anything else, she gives me this distant look or just gets up and leaves the room."

"She's still trying to cope, Kenneth," Harry said. But it was hard to get the words out. He missed her. "It's only been a few months now. She still needs time to mourn her loss."

"I'm not sure you're right about that," Kenneth replied, a grim note entering his voice. "Her mourning, I mean. I get the impression it's all locked up somewhere deep inside, and she's fighting as hard as she can to keep it there."

They walked on awhile before Kenneth added, "Our pastor has talked to me several times since the funeral about a visit. He gave me another call yesterday. I told Patrick that Kyle was going to church with Abigail, and he said he was glad to hear it. But he thinks he should stop by."

"Can't be a bad thing," Harry assured him. "She hasn't seen him since the funeral, right? It's bound to be time."

"I wish I knew for sure," Kenneth replied, still doubtful.

Harry was struck by a sudden thought. "Hey, why

don't you invite Abigail over for supper at our place? You and Kyle, too."

Kenneth turned to him. "Are you serious?"

"Sure, why not? Give Martha a chance to see how our little girl is doing. Or at least hear about her from Abigail." Harry liked the sudden light in Kenneth's eyes. "Who knows, maybe Kyle will actually join us. Can't hurt to try."

The pastor's visit started off even worse than Kenneth had feared. Patrick Langdon had led the church since Kenneth's arrival in Washington nine years earlier. He was a friend to Kenneth and Kyle both, had married them and helped found Joel's mission. He had been an integral part of their lives right through the baby's illness. Seeing him finally seated again in their living room after so long an absence only made the difference between their lives then and now that much clearer—and so much harder to bear.

And Kyle. She sat at the edge of her seat, the teacup and saucer balanced on her knees. She wore one of her new dresses she always seemed to be buying nowadays with Abigail. It was flashy and modern, with a hemline far too short for Kenneth's taste. The bold colors did not match the reserved demeanor in her eyes or voice as she asked, "Will you have more tea?"

"No thank you." Patrick was one of those ageless men, tall and energetic and boyish. His face remained unlined even as he approached his fiftieth year, and his sandy blond hair did not seem to gray as much as simply become transparent. He had already tried to engage Kyle in several different subjects, but without success. Kenneth could almost feel his frustration as he tried again. "I was down at the mission this morning, Kyle. They're being overwhelmed. Joel and Ruthie certainly could use your help."

She lifted her cup and touched it to her lips. "I'm sure they're doing fine without me."

Patrick leaned forward, his voice gentle but direct. "Perhaps it would do you some good, Kyle."

Her gaze sharpened. "You're sure about that?"

"Perhaps it would help you to get out, to reach outside yourself—"

"I'm out all the time. I couldn't possibly be much busier." She made an event of checking her watch. "As a matter of fact, we really will need to cut this short or I'll be late for another meeting."

"Kyle," the pastor started, then hesitated. He glanced at Kenneth.

Kenneth returned the glance but said nothing. There was little he could do here. The whole encounter went just as he had feared. He felt himself sitting at a distance, watching them like he would actors on a stage—his friend struggling to offer the love and support Kyle had refused to accept from him or their families or anyone else. Kenneth lowered his gaze and offered a simple prayer to God.

"Kyle," Patrick repeated, "there's an empty place in our hearts—in our church. I would love to—"

"I have decided it would do me good to attend another church for a while. We're planning to attend my mother's church downtown one Sunday very soon."

"I'm glad to hear that." The pastor's tone was warm and genuine. "At this difficult time in your lives, hearing God's Word and fellowshipping with His family is vital for keeping a strong connection to Him and His love."

Kyle's hands grew agitated, and the cup was nervously set down on the center table. "How kind of you to say so."

"Kyle." Again there was the hesitation, then, "Have

you given thought to filling the void in your lives with another child?"

She was on her feet so fast neither man realized she had actually moved. "I really must be on my way," she said as if Patrick had not spoken.

He drew out his own rising, taking enough time to courageously finish his thought. "I have seen this happen before, I am sorry to say. And I also have seen how the grieving can be shortened, how emotions are made whole by having a reason to look forward and not—"

Kyle stopped him by thrusting out her hand into the air between them. "Thank you so much for stopping by." The courtesy of the words did not extend to her eyes.

Patrick sighed and accepted her hand. "I will continue to pray for you both, Kyle."

Kenneth followed him outside, closing the door behind them. "I'm very sorry, Patrick. I apologize for Kyle. . . ." He drifted to a stop, then turned to go back inside in defeat.

"On the way over here, I was remembering the first time you brought her to church," the pastor said quietly, stopping Kenneth with his words. "I had never seen a woman's eyes shine so."

"She had the gaze of an excited little child," Kenneth agreed. The memory was enough to tear open all the wounds, all the yearnings for what had been. "It was one of the first things I noticed about her, and one of the characteristics I loved most."

Patrick offered Kenneth his hand. "You must please let me know if there's anything at all I can do."

Kenneth silently walked to the sidewalk with him and watched until the man had disappeared around the corner, then sighed and returned to the house. As he put his hand on the doorknob, an unexpected peace filled his soul. "She is yours first, Lord, not mine. Help me to love her like you do."

He found Kyle pacing angrily back and forth across the living room. "How *dare* that man say such a thing to me."

"He was only trying to help."

"I don't want his help!" Her heels jabbed at the carpet with each step, as though she wanted to drill through the floor. "I don't want another baby! I want *my* baby!"

"I know, honey. So do I." To his surprise, Kenneth did not feel disturbed by the outburst. "I wish I could do something, change the hands of time or make it all better. If I could, I would."

She did not seem to have heard him. "I want *my* baby. Not another one. *Never* another one." Then her pacing began to slow. Her face started to lose its tautness, as though internal strings were loosening.

She stopped in the middle of the room and whispered to the emptiness surrounding her, "I'll never go through this pain again. I can't."

"I know," he said, stepping forward, reaching out, drawing her near. Feeling her respond and soften and fold onto his chest for the first time in months. Hearing her softly sob. For a moment at least her isolation had been breached.

Kenneth raised his hand and softly stroked her hair. He leaned over and kissed the top of her head, full of gratitude that for now, for this tiny instant, his wife was back again. He loved her, this woman-child whose heart seemed too fragile for the burden she was being forced to bear.

But even as he held her, he knew the journey back was far from over yet.

CHAPTER FOURTEEN

JOEL AWOKE FEELING BETTER than he had in weeks, well enough to brave the chill dawn air and help with what had come to be known at the center as the morning patrol. It was a good time to search out new faces, while the young wanderers were still huddled under blankets or sleeping inside the limping vehicles which had brought them to the city.

The area of Washington known as Adams Morgan was a place in transition. On the fringe of Washington life, it was full of little artsy coffeehouses and run-down warehouses and corners of immigrant population. In recent times it was also being flooded by young people.

At the front entrance to a derelict tenement, Joel noticed a shadow that didn't quite fit with the other street shadows. Approaching the area, he realized he was looking at two bodies huddled together under a tattered overcoat. Joel cleared his throat, and one of the heads emerged, then the other. A boy and a girl, probably thirteen and fifteen and maybe brother and sister, though they were so dirty it was hard to tell, stared back at him. One of the things that worried him so about these new street kids was how they seemed to be getting younger all the time.

"Good morning," he said, keeping his tone carefully matter-of-fact. He could see from their gazes that smiles would not be trusted. Not from a stranger. "My name is Joel. I'm from the Morning Glory Center. It's a place where you can come for a meal, a shower, or a bed if you want it. Have you eaten recently? How about some hot soup?"

Joel caught the tiniest flicker of interest from the hollow eyes. He went on to tell them that the Center had a doctor, they could stay as long or as short as they wished, and they could make a free call home.

"Or I can do it for you," he explained, knowing the litany of information was less important than assuring them of his genuine care. "You can listen in while I let your folks know you're okay. I won't tell them where you are unless you want me to."

The introduction to the Center was by now so familiar that Joel could keep his mind fastened upon his heart and the prayers he was forming. He offered his hand. "Would you like to come in and get warm?"

Joel led the pair back through the narrow street in silence. He knew it would take time and prayer and patience before they would be ready to hear anything else he had to say.

When the mission came into view, he heard a little gasp from the girl and it made him smile. The ancient brick facade was whitewashed, then decorated with sunny flowers. They stretched up two stories, blooming in giant profusion the entire length of the block. In the feeble light of a cold January morning, the effect was stunning.

Over the entrance, the words "Morning Glory" had been painted in bright gold letters four feet high. Higher still a sun resembling a four-pointed cross beamed down upon the tattered street scene.

Gingerly the ragged pair followed him across the street and up the mission's crumbling steps. Inside, Joel smiled a greeting to a group of long-haired hippies waiting for the breakfast line to open. Joel turned the two over to a gentle young woman who volunteered three mornings a week and had a very soft touch with frightened newcomers. He was about to go set up for the morning prayer service when a familiar voice called his name.

Joel turned to greet the doctor hurrying over, a serious young man who volunteered his medical services two mornings a week. He was also their family doctor. He greeted Joel with, "Why didn't you come in for the tests?"

"I got caught up with work. We're so understaffed these days, and there are more kids all the time."

"And they are working you to death." His dark eyes flashed with more than professional care. "Have you told Ruthie yet?"

"I can't. She's up at the farm again. They're really having financial troubles, and——"

"This can't wait any longer, Joel. You have to prepare her."

He hated these conversations. Hated the tension, the certainty of the prognosis but the uncertainty of *when*. Joel offered a feeble protest. "I've been feeling good recently."

"You and I both know these temporary ups and downs don't mean a thing." The finality of the words were softened by his underlying concern. "When does she get back?"

"Saturday afternoon."

"I'm here for another clinic Monday morning. I want to hear you have spoken to her by then, all right?" He made sure the unspoken warning was understood before asking, "How is Ruthie doing?"

"Fine. The baby is kicking up a storm."

"Then you don't have any reason to delay this."

Joel sighed his defeat. "I'll tell her."

"As soon as she's back, Joel." Again there was the hard edge to his gaze. "I will help you if it's necessary."

Joel sat across the table from his wife. Their apartment and the center's offices covered the fourth floor. The third floor was split in two, half holding rooms for overnight volunteers and half for young people. The second floor contained more dorm rooms and places for two more staff. The ground floor was divided into chapel, clinic, and public rooms.

Their apartment was furnished in the same mismatched donations as the mission. Joel was usually too filled with the happiness and shared purpose of their days to notice. But now he sat and looked around the kitchen and saw how no two chairs at their table matched, how the refrigerator door was held shut with string, how the stove only had one burner that functioned. He could not keep a sigh from escaping.

Ruthie looked up from knitting a tiny cap. "What's the matter?"

He looked down at the Bible, open and unread before him. "I was just wishing I could give you more than I do."

"Oh. That again." She smiled as the needles clicked cheerfully. "You just want me to tell you how happy I am."

He looked at his wife, saw the traces of fatigue left over from her trip to the farm. In her condition, the journeys took a lot out of her. But she felt it important that she be there for the family in their time of need. "How was everything up there?"

It took her a moment to respond. "Well, Simon and Patience, they are seeing much of one another. Every time I am around Patience, I am surprised by how much she is like Mama."

"That's exactly what I thought."

"She and Simon and Sarah have been working on something. Nobody knows exactly what. But they've taken over Mama's tool shed and they won't let anybody in."

Joel repeated, more softly this time, "How was everything?"

"Hard." The needles slowed as the shadow came and went across her face. "I don't know how they are going to make ends meet, but Papa promises it will be all right. With the Lord's help."

Joel closed the Book and set it on the table. He didn't want to do this, but the doctor was coming back the next morning, and Joel knew if he didn't say anything, the doctor might say it for him. "Ruthie, I have some news of my own."

She took one look at his face, and the needles stopped. "You've seen the doctor?"

Joel nodded and watched as her movements turned very deliberate. Carefully she folded up her knitting and settled it on the table by his Bible. When her hands were nestled in her lap, he explained. "He says I have to stop doing so much."

"The same I have been saying, and more." Her accent thickened as it always did when she was worried. "Glad I am he has said what needs saying."

"He wants me to stop doing everything." There. It was finally out. Though just forming the words tore at him. "He says it's the only way."

"Did he say . . ." She had to stop and swallow. "Your heart?"

He did not want to speak the words. He did not want to cause her more worry. Not now. Not ever. But the doctor was right. She had to know. "He says it's gotten worse."

"Then this must we do," Ruthie replied with forced firmness. "Rest you must, and stop with the moving and cleaning and such as that."

"But there's so much—"

"And so many who will help, and so much we shall turn over to God."

He dropped his head. "I love the ministry so much."

She reached over and took his hands with her own. "My beloved husband, still you can give the best of what you have. Your words and your love of God, those are still yours to give." She waited until he raised his gaze to meet her own. Love and concern and pride filled her eyes and shone from her face. "Speak from the heart, my husband. Let other hands do the other work. Be happy with what still is ours."

"All right," he agreed, loving her all the more.

"Stay healthy and here with me," Ruthie said, her eyes glistening. He saw her try for a smile. "I want our baby to know what a wonderful man is his papa."

CHAPTER FIFTEEN

ABIGAIL PACED BACK AND FORTH along the church's broad top step, thinking to herself that everything was finally going according to plan.

Kyle had put her off about actually attending a church service together—she'd said something about a pastor's visit that had upset her terribly. Abigail had not been able to gather much more from either Kenneth or Kyle. She only knew that time after time Kyle had postponed their coming, until finally this week she had agreed. Probably more to placate her than anything else, she realized.

The weather was splendid, a brilliant day with the temperature still crisp enough to require a winter coat. Abigail absently stroked her fur as she waited. The sunshine and bright blue sky showed the church at its best. It truly was an impressive building, all aged stone and large arches and tall mahogany doors. She smiled and waved as she spotted the two approaching. Yes, it really was just as she had imagined, with all her friends there to greet them and see Abigail enter with her fine young daughter and son-in-law. Just like she had always planned it.

But as she walked forward to embrace them, she wondered why she felt a sense of disquiet, as though the perfect day had suddenly sounded a distant but improper chord.

"Hello, my dear. How are you today?"

"Fine, thank you, Mother. You look lovely."

Again there was that jarring discord. She held Kyle at arm's length, long enough to give her daughter a swift inspection. Kyle looked fine, impeccably dressed as usual these days, with every hair in place. Sunglasses hid her eyes, and the rest of Kyle's face was as impersonal as the glasses. Abigail could not understand why she was feeling unsettled.

She turned to her son-in-law. "Hello, Kenneth."

His smile was genuine. Maybe a bit weary, but from the heart. And something more. "Thank you for your invitation, Abigail."

"You are most welcome." Whatever was there in Kenneth's gaze left her feeling the sense of unease even more strongly. She turned them around. "Come along, I really must introduce you to some of my friends."

Their walk through the foyer and into the vestibule became a slow procession, as Abigail did her best to introduce everyone she knew. Kyle handled it with formal precision, something about her manner continuing to trouble Abigail. Kenneth, on the other hand, held none of the reserve she would have expected to find. She knew he would have preferred returning to their old church. Yet here he was, smiling and at ease, allowing her to pull them from one person to the next, showing remarkable grace. And something more. What was it?

Eventually they made their way down to Abigail's spot, a pew on the left just over halfway down. She waved to a few other familiar faces, then settled herself between Kyle and Kenneth. As soon as he was seated, Kenneth bowed his head and closed his eyes.

Abigail turned to her daughter and said, "Did we buy that dress together?"

"No, I picked it out last week. Do you like it? It's from the latest Chanel collection."

Then it hit her. Hard. Abigail opened her mouth, but no words came. *She sounds exactly like me.* The thought struck her with the force of a blow, made even more powerful by how self-evident it now seemed. As though she had been seeing it for months but refusing to recognize it. Yet now, here in church, she found herself looking at Kyle and seeing her with a clarity that could not be denied.

"Mother?"

Still Abigail remained held by the revelation. Kyle was becoming *exactly* like her. Seeing her daughter in this light was most jarring. The correctness and the cool politeness of which Abigail was so proud seemed false and discordant in her daughter.

"Are you all right?"

"Fine," she managed, though the word sounded strangled to her own ears. Kyle had lost what was most precious, the childlike openness and brightness. In its place she was building what Abigail had always wanted and demanded from her, yet which now seemed utterly, totally wrong.

But all she could say right then was, "You look very nice, dear."

Abigail watched as Kyle turned back to the church bulletin, yet she knew Kyle was seeing nothing at all. The sunglasses were off, but the eyes still maintained such barriers that nothing could get through. Not even light.

Abigail turned away but found no comfort in glancing about the beautiful sanctuary. She returned a few more smiles and waves, but the new insight into her daughter, the lack of rightness, held her fast.

Her gaze fell upon Kenneth. He still sat with his head

bowed. A quietness stronger than the silence around them seemed to emanate from him, a peace so strong that it began to press in around her. It was profoundly unfamiliar, this peace, and yet she did not draw away. Even when the pastor approached the podium and began the service, even when they stood and sang and sat and listened to the Word, through it all she felt the peaceful acceptance surrounding her son-in-law.

She wondered why it left her feeling so threatened.

After the service Kyle was drawn away by an acquaintance who wanted to continue the introductions. Abigail held back, wanting a word with Kenneth. When they had moved farther down the aisle, she said quietly, "You seemed so, well, at rest back there."

He looked at her a moment, then said, "I had a remarkable thing happen to me a while ago."

She smiled as someone called a greeting but kept her face turned toward Kenneth. "Please, I would like to hear about it."

"Actually, it happened at a time when I was feeling more discouraged and hopeless about Kyle than I ever had before. But God in His mercy gave me a gift, something I wasn't even asking for right then." He paused a moment and looked into the distance as if searching for the next words. "The Lord filled my heart with a peace that is helping me to leave my concerns and fears about Kyle with Him."

Abigail stared at him a moment, then said, "What do you mean?"

"I know. It's difficult for me to understand, too. And I'm certainly still very concerned. Sometimes I get so troubled and impatient it just seems unbearable. But then something happens." A gentle smile touched his lips. "Maybe telling you about yesterday would help."

"Yes, do."

"We had an argument—again. Over nothing, as usual."

"Oh, I'm so sorry." She inspected his face. "You'll excuse me if I say you don't seem upset about it."

"I'm really not. Not anymore. It hurt a lot at the moment. It started over my having to go to the office on a Saturday. You know we have that board meeting on Monday. But then some other things started coming out. Kyle accused me of not having prayed hard enough to save the baby."

Abigail pulled him into an empty pew, away from the crowd. "Kenneth, that's simply awful."

"Yes. But you know, it didn't seem to bother me nearly as much as you might expect. There've been other times like that recently."

"Keep going," she urged. Maybe here would be found the reason for her own unsettled feelings.

"Well, on one side it hurt terribly to have her say that. But on another side, it didn't hurt at all." His eyes took on a distant look. "That gift from God, that peace, seems to crowd out the pain and the worry."

She felt like shaking him, not understanding her own tension. "Yes?"

He smiled apologetically. "Yesterday after I had finished reading a Scripture passage—actually, it was about the time when the Lord and His disciples were in a boat during a storm. His disciples were almost out of their minds with fear, and he lay there *sleeping*. Anyway, I was sitting there, not really praying or anything. And there in the silence I had the impression that it was all going to be okay. That everything Kyle has been trying to keep hidden deep inside was going to come out and be healed." He paused a moment, then finished, "That we would be a family again."

His quiet confidence flew directly in the face of everything they had experienced during those endless months. And yet Abigail could not contradict him. Not even when she felt the sense of challenge and unease rising again within herself. "Kenneth . . ."

"I know, it doesn't seem likely when we see her like this," he said. But the smile he gave Abigail held a sweet fragrance of earlier, happier times. "But it is very *real*, and I believe God is at work—in me and in Kyle."

Still she felt no closer to understanding. As though she was being given a vital message, spoken in a voice too quiet for her to hear. "I'm very glad for you."

"Yes." His gaze shifted to somewhere behind her, and Abigail knew Kyle was approaching. Then he looked back to her and said, "Have you given any more thought to Martha and Harry's dinner invitation?"

She was about to put him off again, as she had done several times already over the past few weeks. But this time something held her back. Some quiet inkling that here might be what she was searching for. Which of course was impossible. Whatever could she, a woman of society, find in the home of a couple like that?

Kyle appeared at her elbow, "Are we ready to go?"

Abigail looked at her daughter's carefully composed facade, and then back at the quiet, peaceful confidence which surrounded Kenneth. Impossible that he could have so much hope. Impossible that things could return to how they were before.

But she found herself saying to Kenneth, "Tell them I would love to come."

To an observer, the room held a scene of domestic tranquility. A warm fire crackled in a hearth almost too large for the cozy living room. Cups of evening tea sat on the small table before them. Kenneth sat with his slippered feet resting on a footstool, his tie removed and thrown over the back of his chair, while he read the paper.

Kyle, in a soft fleecy cotton robe, occupied the opposite chair. A piece of stitchery was held firmly in one slender hand as the needle plied back and forth, tracing out the design.

Earlier, Kenneth had made occasional comments, snippets of local news or an item of business at the office. Long before that he had exhausted all inquiries concerning her own day. There was little for Kyle to share. Her activities had simply been like all the others before that. Besides, she did not feel like talking. It was hard enough to manage a polite nod to Kenneth's comments. Now they sat in silence, each occupied with unspoken thoughts.

Kyle's needle threaded back and forth through the material. As unwelcome as small talk seemed to be, she was not comfortable with the silence either. Despite the fire, the room felt cold to her. Though they sat only a few feet apart, the distance between their souls was immeasurable. It was an awkward, unpleasant feeling. Cool. Remote. Lonely.

What made things worse was that Kenneth did not seem aware of any awkwardness. A swift little glance in his direction reaffirmed what she had been noticing for some time now. A kind of peace had descended upon him. She was not sure she liked it. Why shouldn't he be suffering the same isolation and emptiness as she was? The feeling of calm emanating from him was like a silent challenge.

Perhaps it was good that the baby . . . A child would be bound to feel her emptiness. . . .

Kyle checked herself. If they had not lost the baby, she

herself would not be feeling so empty.

Suddenly Kyle thought of Martha. Was this how it had been for Martha and Harry, her parents? Two people, shut away from each other by their hurt and loss, struggling to keep each day's small events from completely overwhelming them? And then Joel. Surely he had suffered most of all, emotionally isolated as he was from the two of them. It was a wonder he had turned out as whole, as giving as he had.

Well, she couldn't turn to them, or to any of Ruthie's family for that matter. She could not even turn to Kenneth. Once she would have done so in a heartbeat. Such a long, long time ago. She couldn't now. Kyle wasn't quite sure how it had happened, but the door was closed. A great distance now lay between them. She found herself wondering if perhaps the emptiness had always been in her, and all her earlier joy and satisfaction with her life had just been a myth. Perhaps they had lived in a fantasy world, one that was bound to crash in on them. She felt as though she did not even know Kenneth any longer. But then, she didn't know herself, either.

Another brief glance assured her that Kenneth was still reading, though she had not heard the rustle of the paper for many minutes. Even the ticking mantel clock seemed to be holding its breath, not willing to break the heavy silence.

Kyle could take it no more. She laid her needlework aside and rose to her feet. "I think I'll be off to bed."

Kenneth glanced at the clock. "It's only a few minutes past eight."

She knew he disliked long evenings spent alone. No matter that her company these days was not much better. "I'll go up and read in bed for a while."

He put the paper aside and gave Kyle his full attention.

"I do wish you'd come with Abigail and me for supper with Harry and Martha."

"I told you I'd think about it," she responded, but her tone said no.

"How about bringing your book down here? It's nice and cozy here by the fire."

Cozy. Hardly. Kyle felt stifled, yet strangely alone. Kenneth's eyes held her, seeming both to plead and to reach out. She turned from the look. She could not bear it. She merely shook her head in reply and started for the door.

"Good night, then."

Kyle mumbled good night in return and hastily made her way up the stairs. She felt she was fleeing from this strange yet compelling sense of peace surrounding Kenneth.

But once in bed, she could not read. The words blurred on the page. Impatiently she set the book aside. What was happening to her? It had all been so different before. . . . Kyle shook away the thought and all the memories that she could not bring up again. Not ever.

But the image of her husband, so calm, so patient, would not be erased from her mind. Almost as though he waited for her to come back from some distant journey. He had aged; yes, the strain was there in his face. He too had lost a child, and it showed. Yet he still had something— she was not sure what it was. Maybe life. And she . . . she had nothing. Her days were just as empty and as meaningless as her nights. They blurred together into a long gray highway that stretched out behind her and endlessly before her. And there was no one who could understand, really understand. No one.

Kyle dropped her book to the floor and turned off the

light. She buried her face in the pillow and fought back sudden tears. "No more," she quietly promised herself. No more tears. No more grief.

She was fine.

CHAPTER SIXTEEN

"ABIGAIL. HOW NICE TO SEE YOU." The graying member of Rothmore Insurance's Board of Directors gave her a smile and brisk handshake. "What brings you up here today?"

"I have a meeting with Kenneth."

"So did I. We've just spent the entire morning going over some figures." He pointed toward the boardroom down by her husband's former office. Through the open door she could see Kenneth gathering up reams of paper. "He managed to answer every one of my questions without a hitch."

"How does he seem to you?"

Mr. Dixon examined her. They had known each other a long time. "Are you talking about Kenneth the rising company executive, or Kenneth the young man?"

"Both, I suppose."

"The company is in good hands, Abigail. I mean that sincerely." All traces of humor had evaporated from the senior executive's voice. "I was worried for a while, of course. But he is bright, dedicated, and a born leader. He is going to make us a good chief executive sometime soon.

I am becoming more convinced of that every day."

Generally the man was rather miserly with his praise. She should have been very satisfied to hear such a glowing report. But the same niggling feeling she'd had in church returned. She felt there was something she was missing, something vital. "And personally?"

"That," Mr. Dixon replied slowly, "is harder to put into words."

Kenneth looked up from his sorting and spotted her. He waved and called, "Be right with you, Abigail."

"Take your time, dear," she replied, then lowered her voice to say to Mr. Dixon, "Try. Please."

"Very well." He looked away a moment, then back at Abigail's face. "I think Kenneth Adams is growing into someone I can only admire from afar."

"I beg your pardon?" Of all the things the graying gentleman could have said, nothing could have surprised her more.

"You don't have to look hard to see how tough these past months have been for him. How long has it been since his child died, five months? Six?"

"Almost seven," Abigail replied quietly, not needing to count the passing days. "Seven next week, in fact."

"I have four children of my own and six grandchildren. For a while I couldn't meet his eye. That's the truth. He was living through my own worst nightmare. I thought for a while it would crush him. What he has endured would have done me in, and that's for sure."

"But it didn't, not Kenneth," Abigail said, aching for her daughter and for her son-in-law.

"No. It didn't." His gaze reached through the open door and rested on Kenneth as he finished tidying up. His words stumbled as he tried to form ideas he had not fully shaped in his mind. "He has been broken, yes, and now he is being reshaped. That's just my own impression, mind you. But there's something about him, something new. A calm—no, not just a calm."

"I think I understand."

"Serene, that's it," the man said, satisfied with himself for finding the word. "The man is serene. Sure, he's still in pain from an incredible loss. But I'm seeing something new in him. A surprising depth." He hesitated a long moment. "It's something other than simply a coping mechanism. But I really don't know what it is or where it comes from." He paused again. "It challenges me."

Abigail murmured, "You too?"

Only once did Abigail interrupt the silence on the journey out to the Grimes' home. "Do you still feel confident about things working out with Kyle?" she asked, staring out the passenger-side window with unseeing eyes.

"Yes." The response did not need to be loud to convey its strength. "Yes, I do."

Abigail settled back with a sigh. She saw no need to ask if he was still finding his own comfort and peace. Kenneth's calm blanketed the car, while at the same time she felt an accusatory finger pointed straight at her. She did not understand why she felt that way, but she did.

Kenneth pulled down a side street of modest postwar houses, all set within little postage-stamp lots. Abigail asked, "Is this where they live?"

"Just up here on the right."

The house was similar to the others, standing neat and freshly painted at the top of a lawn which rose like three green steps. She peered through the window as Kenneth pulled up and stopped, then murmured, "Maybe this isn't such a good idea after all."

"It'll be fine," Kenneth assured her.

She looked down at her designer linen and silk outfit. "I'm quite certain I could not have worn anything more inappropriate."

"A bathing suit could have topped it," Kenneth joked and got a small smile out of her. "No, really, you look fine."

She waited while he came around to open the door for her. Abigail stepped onto the sidewalk and looked around uncertainly. They were miles from anywhere she knew.

"Hello! How nice to see you!" Martha Grimes allowed the front door to close behind her and hurried down the walk. "Isn't this exciting?"

"Yes, terribly," Abigail agreed dryly, watching Kenneth over Martha's shoulder as she returned the woman's embrace. Kenneth only smiled back warmly.

Martha released her to turn and hug Kenneth. "Hello, Kenneth, dear. How are you?"

"Better every day," he replied, his tone genuine.

"I'm so glad." Martha took a step back and looked down the walk, then glanced in the car. "She wouldn't come?"

"No, I'm sorry." Kenneth's tone was impossibly gentle. "I warned you she probably wouldn't."

"Yes, you did." The sorrow was evident in Martha's voice. "But I couldn't help hoping."

"You mustn't take it personally, Martha."

Abigail's heart went out to the woman. She slipped her arm through Martha's and drew her close. "You were so nice to have me over. I can't thank you enough."

The distraction worked. Martha dabbed at her eyes and smiled around her regret. "Oh, nonsense. After all the

126

wonderful places you've been, our little home is going to be awfully simple—"

"There is no place as grand as one filled with love and friendship," Abigail quickly said. As Martha led her toward the house, Abigail caught sight of Kenneth's startled expression. She agreed with him wholeheartedly. She had no idea either where those words had come from.

The home's interior was about what she had expected, threadbare carpet and worn-out furniture. Yet the little touches of color and homeyness gave their place a warmth and cheer which surprised Abigail.

The genuine welcome in Martha's greeting was there in Harry's eyes. His "Hello, Abigail" was a bit awkward but said with rough charm. He was wearing what she supposed was his only tie, doing his best to make her feel at home. Which she did. It amazed her how comfortable she felt. Even when they led her down the narrow hallway to the kitchen and seated her at the table right there by the back door, she felt as much at home as she ever did. The conversation quickly became effortless, and the contentment was solid and real.

The fare was simple but fresh and well prepared. Throughout the dinner, the four of them were united by their consciousness of the empty chair, the quiet absence of the one person who had drawn them all together. They covered it as best they could. There was no need to say a word.

Afterward Abigail tried to rise and help clear away the dishes, but Martha would not hear of it. Martha set everything in the sink, then pulled a steaming pie from the oven. She turned and said, "I hope you like peach cobbler."

"I normally don't permit myself dessert, but tonight I believe I will indulge," Abigail replied with a smile. "I haven't had peach cobbler in—oh, it must be years."

"Shucks," Kenneth quipped. "I was hoping to have yours."

After a shared laugh, Harry commented, "Bet you've never eaten in a place like this before."

"No," Abigail agreed ruefully. "It probably would have done me some good if I had."

There was a moment's quiet after dessert, the room so still Abigail could hear the coffee percolating. But there was no discomfort. Silence at a table was something she had been taught to fill. Yet here there was no need. Not for empty chatter, nor for masks, nor for the many things she had always counted as essential to her life.

Her eye was caught again by the empty chair resting at the back wall. If only Kyle had been with them this evening. Her heart felt a sudden spasm of pain as she watched Martha excuse herself to get the coffee. What Martha had lost, and found, and now lost again brought tears to Abigail's eyes.

When Martha returned with the coffee, she noticed Abigail at once. She reached across and took her hand. "What's the matter, my dear?"

"Oh, nothing, I'm all right." She took a shaky breath, gathering herself. "The past is a little too close right now."

"Funny," Harry said, looking around the kitchen. "It can happen to me here in this room more than any other place."

"We all have sorrows and regrets," Martha said. "I wish . . ." But she didn't finish the thought.

"You don't know the things I've done against you," Abigail shakily confessed. "You can't imagine."

"It doesn't matter," Harry said. "Not a bit."

"Yes, it does. It always will."

"It can't." Martha spoke the words with a confidence and strength that brought Abigail up short. "Excuse me, but you are just indulging yourself, Abigail. Are you listening to me? The Lord lets go of our mistakes. They are not remembered. They are cast as far from us as the east is from the west. And we are told by the blessed Lord Jesus to forgive others as we would like the Lord to forgive us. So you and I must do the same."

"Let it go," Harry agreed. "We have."

She looked from one face to the other, saw the deep lines of hard-won lessons. "You sound so . . . well, holy."

That brought a smile and a shared look between the two of them. Harry asked his wife, "Ever think we'd hear somebody call us that?"

"Not in a million years," Martha replied.

Harry turned to Abigail. "It's something how right now we've got all this pain and worry over both our children— Kyle with her heartache and Joel with his heart. It keeps us up nights, I can tell you that. But at the same time . . ." He looked back at his wife. "Maybe you'd better finish."

"You're doing just fine, dear," she prompted. "Go ahead."

"I'm not so good with words," Harry apologized. "I guess all I'm trying to say is that even here in the midst of all this, we can feel the Lord's hand at work. He uses even the bad times, helping us to grow, to reach out to Him, to trust Him to find the way through."

Martha grasped her hand once more. "Let it go, my dear. Let the Lord work in you as He has in us."

Abigail forced herself to smile and nod. But all she could think was how fast these two seemed to be growing, and how wise. Like Kenneth. And there she was, left standing still, lost somewhere far behind.

CHAPTER SEVENTEEN

KYLE WAS COMING DOWN THE STAIRS as the door-
bell rang. She stifled a cry of frustration. It had taken her
two days to work up the nerve to make this little journey.
She knew she had to see Joel and Ruthie's new baby.

She walked to the door, ready with words to swiftly
turn away whomever it might be. Then she opened it and
found herself staring into Martha Grimes' face. Kyle took
a surprised step back. "What. . . ?"

"Hello, dear." The lack of a welcome did not seem to
faze Martha. She entered the front hallway. "How are
you?"

"I'm . . . I'm fine." Kyle wondered if there was some
way the family had learned of her intentions for that day.
No, no. It was not possible. "I'm also in a hurry."

"I won't keep you." The sadness and the caring were
etched into Martha's every feature. "I decided that I
couldn't wait any longer for an invitation. I was over at the
hospital seeing my new grandson and decided to stop by.
I needed to see our daughter again."

Kyle felt a shudder go through her. Forcefully she
pushed it all aside. "I've just need some time alone."

"I understand. You're still struggling, aren't you?"

Martha's statement was said in a straightforward manner that rankled Kyle. "Don't you think I deserve to be sad and upset?"

"No, I do not."

The answer was so direct and forceful that it caused Kyle's head to jerk upright. She stared at her long-lost mother.

"No," Martha repeated just as stoutly. She reached for Kyle's hand, her eyes seeming to plead with Kyle to listen well and understand her words. "No. You do not deserve to draw your pain and grief deep inside you. You are too fine a person, Kyle. Too loving. You have suffered enough."

Kyle listened as the truth constricted the heart she was trying to protect within its hard shell.

"Your anger, your bitterness, is only bringing you *more* suffering," Martha explained, her voice breaking. "Can't you see? You are permitting this sorrow to grind you down. Destroy your faith. Separate you from the loving comfort of your God. You don't deserve that, Kyle. You don't, and neither does God."

Kyle struggled inwardly as conflicting emotions swirled through her mind. Finally she stiffened her shoulders and forced a brave smile into place. "I'm fine. Really, you shouldn't worry—"

"You're making the same kind of mistake I made all those years ago," Martha quietly pleaded, her voice hollow and pain in her eyes. "You're trying to hold everything in, lock it all inside, and bear it alone."

Kyle withdrew her hand and mentally shook herself free of all emotional encumbrances. "I'm fine," she insisted again.

"Let God back in," Martha said once more as she allowed Kyle to usher her outside and down the front steps. "Let God help you."

"I'm fine," Kyle repeated. She felt that if she had to smile much longer her face would crack. "Thank you for stopping by."

The handkerchief in Kyle's lap was twisted into a damp knot. She sat on the edge of the bench and looked up and down the hospital corridor. Would Joel never leave? She did not know why she was there except that it was expected of her.

But she did not want to encounter her brother as well. It was already too much. Part of her wanted to flee from the hospital with its smells and its sounds. She had not been in a hospital since . . . She could not think of that. Not now.

Again she glanced down the corridor, willing Joel to come out the door. He should turn left, away from where she sat, and go down the stairs and out the doors and leave her free to go in and see the baby.

But the corridor remained empty.

She glanced at her watch, angry at her brother for making her wait, furious with them all for . . . for what? She couldn't sort out all the conflicting emotions that drew her one way and then the other. Kenneth had invited her to join him yesterday when he came for his own first meeting with Samuel Harry Grimes. Kenneth had told her yesterday that Joel's father was awfully proud that his grandchild carried his name. Kenneth spoke in that mild tone of his, watching her all the time.

Kenneth's calm sometimes made her want to scream

and tear at her hair. She did not know why. She did not understand a lot of things these days. But they didn't matter. Nothing really mattered except just getting through one more day. Which was why she had refused to go with Kenneth yesterday. Seeing the baby and all the family there at the same time was more than she could face.

With an exasperated sigh Kyle sprang to her feet. She would not wait any longer. She started jerkily down the corridor, having to fight herself each step of the way.

She stopped in front of the door and stood there a long moment, twisting the handkerchief. When a nurse passed by and gave her a curious look, she was spurred to release the handkerchief, raise one hand, and knock.

After a moment's silence, Joel appeared in the doorway. His face beamed with surprised delight. "Kyle! Look, Ruthie, it's Kyle!"

"Let her in! Oh, this is wonderful. I prayed you would come and share the moment." Ruthie was there in the bed, her face bright like Joel's, one hand outstretched to greet her.

The other arm cradled a baby.

Kyle forced her legs to carry her across the room, forced one arm to lift. Her hand was taken by Ruthie. She felt herself drawn down and the hand slip up and around her neck. She held herself as stiff as possible, struggling not to touch the bundle.

As soon as she could, Kyle raised herself back up. She wanted to smile. But she couldn't. She just couldn't make the muscles of her face work. She could do nothing but stand there and look down at the little form.

"Would you like to hold him?"

Her headshake was more of a little shudder. Her arms yearned to reach out, even as the wound in her heart held her back.

Joel slipped one arm around her shoulders and said proudly, "Isn't he beautiful?"

"Yes," she whispered, the voice not her own. And he was. A perfectly beautiful baby boy. She saw the look of love and pride and joy pass between Joel and Ruthie, and shuddered again.

She did not know how long she stood there. But finally she realized her silence grew uncomfortable for the two new parents. She could see the glances they exchanged, the ones filled with concern over her. But she did not want their sorrow. So she made a superhuman effort and put on a show of cheeriness. She noted where they could buy nice clothes for the baby, and how pretty the room was, and how good Ruthie looked—all the right things.

Then she glanced at her watch, just like she had seen Abigail do a thousand times when she was ready to leave, and said some words about needing to be off to her next appointment. She permitted herself to be drawn down into another one-armed embrace by Ruthie. The sorrowful concern shone from her eyes and threatened to make Kyle weep. But she held grimly to her composure. She couldn't cry. Not here. Not now. If she did she would never stop.

"I'll walk with you down to the elevators," Joel said, opening the door for her.

Kyle could not marshal enough energy to object. Just then her mind was held by a single bitter thought. Life was so terribly, horribly unfair.

But Joel did not lead her to the elevators. Instead he took her arm and led her to a bench in the side corridor. "Let's sit down here for a moment."

Kyle felt as though her legs could barely support her own weight. She allowed herself to be guided down, and noted Joel's puffing breath as he seated himself beside her. She glanced over. His complexion was worse than the last time she had seen him. The thought made her pause, for it took a moment to recall when that last time was. It may have been months.

"Kyle, I have something to tell you." His tone was gentle but strong. All expressions of the joy he had shown in the room just a moment before were gone. "You need to know something. I hate to burden you further right now, but I am dying."

The words drew her out from behind the veil of her own bitter anguish.

He looked at her with eyes that were both clear and somber. "Yes, of course, we've been talking about it for years. But now the time is actually here. And only a matter of weeks. Months, if I'm lucky." He stopped and forced a ragged breath. His voice dropped until she could barely hear the words, "I won't see my son's first birthday."

Kyle could not speak. Her mouth worked, but the sounds would not come.

Joel paused a moment, then continued, "I don't have time to wait any longer. Some things need to be out in the open, and right now. Watching my own death come closer and closer, and knowing there is nothing I can do about it, has made me view life—and death—in a very different light." Another pause, another breath, this one easier. "Kyle, you have got to let your grief go."

Though said with great care and concern, the words came with great power. "I can't, Joel," she finally managed.

"Yes, you can." The answer was so direct, so forceful, it caused Kyle's head to snap upright. "Yes," Joel repeated. He reached for Kyle's hand, his eyes pleading for Kyle to listen and understand. "You have told yourself so long and so often that you will never recover from the loss of your baby that you don't even hear the truth any longer. But listen, Kyle. God loves you. His Word tells you that. Your own heart would tell you if you would only let it."

Kyle's deep breath and struggle for control filled the air between them.

"You have suffered enough," Joel persisted quietly. "This anger and bitterness is destroying you."

The tears in Joel's eyes and voice tore at her own heart. With a strangled sob, Kyle jumped to her feet and nearly ran down the hospital corridor.

"Look at him!" Kenneth held up the infant for his aunt Kyle to observe. "Have you ever seen a sturdier boy?"

Kyle managed a smile. Little Samuel certainly was the image of a perfect baby. She tentatively reached out a finger and let the chubby hand curl around it. His grip tightened, amazing her that one so small could grasp so firmly.

"He's beautiful," Martha enthused. "Just beautiful."

They were gathered in Joel and Ruthie's apartment over the mission, there to celebrate the mother and child's arrival home from the hospital. Ruthie, pale but happy, lay back against the sofa piled with extra pillows. Her eyes danced with pleasure as she watched her small son being passed from one pair of hands to another.

"I think it's about Papa's turn again," Joel spoke up. "The rest of you have hogged him long enough." He reached for his infant son, then cuddled and whispered to him as he went back over to sit beside Ruthie.

Kenneth repeated a question for what seemed to Kyle to be the umpteenth time. "So the doctor says he's okay? Everything has checked out?"

"More than okay," Ruthie replied again. "Dr. Pearce says he is perfect. All ten fingers and toes. And not one sign of any heart complication."

"He must take after his mother," Joel said, leaning forward to kiss Ruthie's cheek.

"Not necessarily," Kenneth quickly countered. "I talked with the doctor a while back. He said it is not at all uncommon for families, even ones with some possibility of genetic heart problems, to have normal, healthy children. In fact, a problem is more the exception than the rule."

"Dr. Pearce told me the same thing," Joel agreed, his eyes on his child.

"He told Joel we can go right on raising a whole quiver full of healthy babies," Ruthie added, blushing slightly.

Kyle did not join in the little ripple of laughter that circled the room. For one brief moment her heart quickened. Had the doctor really said that? Was it possible. . . ? No, no. She pushed the idea from her. She would not even consider it. The thought alone was far too dangerous. She could not bear the pain again. She could not open old wounds that she was finally managing to keep out of sight and mind most of the time.

Kyle felt eyes glance her way. She refused to meet their gazes and the unspoken questions contained there.

Finally the small baby broke the tension. With a lusty wail he announced that he had had enough of the family for one day. He now wanted time alone with his mother. Nursing. Cuddling. And a chance for a nice nap.

As Ruthie reached for her baby, Kyle rose to her feet and turned toward the door. But she could not tune out the soft motherly whispers of devotion and comfort.

"We'll leave now," Kenneth was saying. "Again, our congratulations. You have a beautiful son, Joel. We wish you—all three—God's blessing."

"He has blessed us," Joel answered, and Kyle could

hear how the emotions turned his voice husky. She could not bear any more.

"Don't forget, we want you to come up just as . . ." Kyle heard Martha's voice fade as she hurried down the steep stairway. The empty landing below echoed her impatient footsteps, and she felt the steps' hollow sound ring all the way up to her heart. She took a breath of the afternoon air and resolved to be firm. She was fine. As long as she kept herself firmly in check, she would make it just fine.

CHAPTER EIGHTEEN

"DID YOU NOTICE HER HAT?"

"Who could help but notice it?" A shared titter followed the comment.

Kyle had entered the church hall, her hands filled with flowers for the upcoming charity tea. She had no idea whom the two ladies were discussing but was relieved it was not her. Fortunately she was not wearing a hat.

"Oh, finally you're here," called a voice to her right. Mrs. Tilly, a member of the decorating committee, hurried toward Kyle, her brightly flowered skirt swishing with each step. "I've been growing anxious."

Kyle nodded. Mrs. Tilly was often anxious.

"Good, you were able to get the deep pink ones like I asked. I was so hoping you could. They will go splendidly with the other decorations." The woman exuberantly scooped up the armful of flowers and disappeared into the side room, talking to herself as she went.

One of the younger women, Molly, screwed up her face as the swishing skirt disappeared. "So how many florists did you visit before you found the deep pink ones?"

Kyle sighed. "Five. I was about to give up."

"I'm sure the deeper pink will make the cakes and tea taste so much better," Molly mimicked, and the young women gathered nearby laughed.

Kyle hung her coat and proceeded over to help with the decorating.

Someone asked Kyle, "Did Abigail come with you today, dear?"

"No, she won't make it," Kyle replied, setting out the dishes. "She's been feeling a little under the weather."

"Oh, nothing serious, I hope."

"No," Kyle said, though she did not know for certain. Abigail refused to discuss her health with anyone.

The conversation swirled onward.

"Kyle, be a dear and go get us another set of tablecloths. You'll find them in the box in the kitchen."

"No she won't. I just saw them in the reception area back by the church offices."

"What on earth are they doing back there?"

"I haven't any idea. There was a box of cutlery there beside it."

"I'll go see," Kyle said, glad for an excuse to leave the chatter behind for a moment. Such gatherings were safe and comfortable, but sometimes the noise and inconsequential chitchat seemed to push at her. As she walked down the long back corridor toward the church offices, Kyle found herself wondering why the event was ever dubbed a charity tea. She knew that by the time the elaborate decorations and fussy luncheon items were paid for, there would be precious little left for charity.

"Kyle, what a pleasant surprise!"

The unexpected voice astounded and dismayed her. The last person she had expected to bump into here at Abigail's church on the day of a charity tea was Reverend Patrick Langdon. She had not seen their former pastor since the day he visited her at the house. Kyle finally managed, "What are you doing here?"

"Why, just paying my colleague a visit. We talk and pray together from time to time." He stepped forward, examining her with that penetrating gaze of his. "How are you doing, Kyle?"

"Fine, I'm fine," she repeated automatically as she backed away from him. His presence here was unnerving, as though her veneer of safety was being penetrated.

Patrick stayed where he was. "We've all missed you. I've asked Kenneth several times if I might come by for another visit."

"We just need a little time." She suddenly felt it very important to include Kenneth. She did not wish to face this intent man baring her own soul. "We are adjusting." Then she added a practiced, pious phrase that she hoped would release her from the careful scrutiny. "God has been good."

"Has He?" The pastor's eyes widened. "So through all the pain and bewilderment of loss, your faith in God and in His love has held firm?"

"Oh yes," she replied quickly.

She sensed he was trying to read whether her true feelings were in keeping with her lips, so she repeated, "God has been good. Joel and Ruthie have a perfect, healthy baby." She stopped, wondering why she had said those words. But there was no taking them back.

"I know you must be happy for them," Patrick said, a hint of a smile speaking of his kind heart. Then he went on slowly, "But it must cause questions for you, as well. Why a healthy baby for them, and not for you?"

Kyle shifted uncomfortably and licked her lips. He was getting far too personal, too direct. She had to speak, had to fill the difficult silence without giving the truth away.

"The doctor said it was not at all uncommon," she explained hurriedly. "He said Joel could likely have a dozen babies—all healthy."

The smile broadened. "That is great news. For you and Kenneth, too."

Kyle knew what he meant. She only nodded, feeling the coldness wrap around her heart.

"We continue to pray for you," the pastor said. "My wife and I, and our prayer group at church, as well. We are asking that God will be there with you in your time of trial and sorrow. That He will lead you in the future, and give you a healthy child—or children—according to His own will and timing."

"Thank you, that is . . ." She could not go on. The man was praying for something she had no intention of ever allowing to happen.

But his gaze remained level upon her. "We also pray that you will accept the inner peace and comfort He is offering."

"That's wonderful . . . thank . . . I really must be going." She fumbled for the box of tablecloths, feeling that there was nothing more important than simply to get away. "I'd best not be taking any more of your time."

"My time is meant to be taken," he said warmly.

"Yes, well, I have things . . . the tea is starting . . . so good to see you." She pushed back through the doors and out into the corridor, trying hard not to run.

The following week, Kyle spent the entire taxi ride home from yet another charity function preparing a list of excuses. She had successfully avoided a visit to Abigail's home since the baby's death. The Rothmore estate held too many memories. Kyle did not need to think out this conclusion. She knew instinctively that a visit to Abigail's home would endanger her carefully preserved barriers. Too much might threaten to break through.

But Abigail had grown peevish over Kyle's continued refusals to visit her home and had offered to host a charity luncheon herself. Kyle knew it was a tactic calculated to force her to come over. And not just for the luncheon itself. Abigail could now insist on Kyle helping her plan the event. And the way she hinted that she was not feeling entirely well was most certainly another part of her scheme. That was just like Abigail.

Also nagging at her mind and emotions was what she had learned the day before—about Joel's health continuing to decline. Kenneth had come home with the news, his complete calm reduced for the first time in weeks. Kyle found herself recalling what Joel had told her in the hospital corridor. And those were things she could not risk thinking about for very long. They threatened to destroy her defenses entirely.

Kyle was so involved in worrying over the luncheon and her brother's health that she was through the hall and up two of the stairs before she realized Kenneth was seated in the living room. She returned to the doorway. "I didn't expect you so early."

Then she saw the doctor rise to his feet.

It was hard for old Dr. Pearce to be threatening. But that was exactly her impression as he turned to her. The tired gray eyes inspected her with such clarity that she was filled with foreboding.

"Hello, Kyle," the doctor said. "I'm glad to see you."

"Join us for a moment, won't you, dear?" Kenneth asked.

Reluctantly she took a single step into the room. "What's the matter?"

"Not a thing, I am very happy to say." Dr. Pearce gestured to the sofa beside him. "Please come have a seat."

She crossed her arms defensively and stayed where she was. Whatever it was that brought the doctor here, she knew it was something she was not going to like.

"Kyle," Kenneth hesitated, then forced himself to continue, "Dr. Pearce and I . . . darling, we have been talking about whether we should have another baby."

"Never." The word was as forceful as if she had stamped her foot.

But Dr. Pearce did not let it go. "You saw little Samuel for yourself," he reminded her. "He is fine. There is no reason for you not to have a healthy baby."

"Why can't you understand?" She felt the rage building but would not let it out. She couldn't. If she did, the pain would come through as well. She heard the steel in her voice as she finished, "I will never have another baby. And that is final."

She turned and left the room, forcing herself to hold to a steady pace but wanting to flee. They would never understand. They couldn't. But she knew that even if the second baby was fine, all the pain of losing Charles would be forced out. Every time she looked at the new child, she would ache for the one who was not there.

Kyle stopped at the top of the stairs and leaned against the wall. The effort to keep it all inside was overwhelming. And what made it far worse, almost too much to bear, was the quiet, insistent voice. The one she could almost always pretend not to hear—until now, when they forced her to listen. It whispered to her in the night, the aching desire deep within to do what they said, to try again. Kyle forced herself erect and walked down to her room. It was impossible.

CHAPTER NINETEEN

THE PHONE CALL CAME AT two o'clock in the morning. Later Kyle had the impression that she had already been awake, lying there waiting for what she somehow knew was coming. Just as she knew that Kenneth would rise and walk down the stairs to take the call in the front hall, not in their bedroom. She walked to the top of the stairs and stood there in her nightgown, watching as he sat down even before he said hello. She knew that he, too, already sensed what was to come.

"Yes." Kenneth listened for one brief second and raised his free hand to hold the side of his face. "Yes. Simon. Hello."

He paused, then, "I see. Yes, of course. No, not at all, thank you. It was very kind to let us know immediately."

Another pause, longer this time, then, "Do you think so? All right. I'll be going over immediately. Yes. I know the hospital. You will? Yes. I have it. I'll be there to meet you. All right. Good-bye."

Kenneth fumbled as he tried to return the receiver to its place without looking. The receiver slipped out of his hand and tumbled to the floor. Kenneth did not reach to set it back. He just sat there, his hand on the side of his face, staring blindly at the opposite wall.

"Kenneth?"

He stirred then, turning slowly, taking his time, finally focusing on her at the top of the stairs. "Prepare yourself, Kyle, my love."

She said the words because she needed to release her breath. But she already knew. "It's Joel, isn't it?"

"Yes," he said. "Yes. It's Joel."

Nothing about Joel's funeral seemed real. The humming of voices and floating of images was the stuff of vague dreams. Kyle was aware of Kenneth's arm supporting her. She knew she was guided into the pew alongside a weeping Martha. She felt Harry reach over and grip her hand for a very long while.

And there was Ruthie. Eyes puffy from crying, clinging to the baby bundled in her arms. Her family surrounded her, buoying her up, reminding her that she was not alone.

Reverend Langdon stepped to the podium, his dark robe well suited to the day. Kyle looked away. She did not want to see his smile meant as assurance to the grieving. Numbly she let the words drift around her without registering.

She wasn't even aware that the service had ended until she felt Kenneth's hand lightly urging her to stand. She followed the casket down the aisle with the rest of the family. The only thing she noticed was Martha holding the baby, and Ruthie being supported by her mother and Simon.

The day was bitterly cold. The cemetery was whipped to a bitter, frozen wasteland by a wind blowing straight from empty northern reaches. The sky was lost behind high clouds like a featureless gray blanket. Kyle chose to stand because she did not want to sit beside the Millers and the Grimeses. She did not want to be that close to their grieving.

She stood slightly around the corner made by the grave and the press of people, tightly hugging her coat against far more than the cold. Her reaction came without thinking now, this need to hold the sorrow and the loss deep inside, so deep she did not even feel it. She stood where she could see the Millers and Harry and Martha all lost together in their grief, and she let them feel for her. The day's single tear froze halfway down her cheek.

Kenneth slipped one arm around her shoulders and raised his other gloved hand to wipe at his cheeks. She knew with a wife's understanding that this time he did not draw her tightly to his side because of her sorrow, but rather because of his own need. For an instant, this realization was almost enough to shatter the walls and pull her out of her shell. All the love she felt for him was pressed down deep inside her as well, she realized in that moment. But as swiftly as that understanding came, she jammed the feelings back down. She could not permit them to arise, not without letting out everything she could not let herself feel. Not ever.

She stood there surrounded by family members and their grief, clenched up tight against the wind and the day and her husband's embrace. An impression arose, and with it a swift keening from the unseen depths of her rigid heart. *So much to hide away.* Then it was as though the bitter wind reached down through the gathering and plucked the thought away.

After the coffin had been lowered, people began to move about, then departed like dark waves of a sea she only half saw. Whispered words about God's will and the kindness of Ruthie having Joel's child were cast about her. Kyle nodded to all that was said, hearing little, seeing less. She felt drained, so exhausted that the walk back to the car seemed endless.

They had buried her brother. One she had only recently come to know. A man she had learned to admire and, yes, to love. Yet she did not feel anything. The realization kept her company on the silent drive home. It had been so long since she had felt anything other than total emptiness.

CHAPTER TWENTY

ONE EVENING IN APRIL Kenneth phoned to say he would not be home at the usual hour, and Kyle had waited to prepare the evening meal. Now as they sat together over the roast, it was Kenneth who opened the conversation.

"I wish there was something more we could do for Ruth. I visited the mission today. Though she didn't say anything, I know Ruth is having a very difficult time."

Kyle lifted her head and felt her heart tugged by painful thoughts. News of Ruth and the small baby was of special interest.

"I'm sure much of it is still so difficult for her." He took a final bite of the roast and put down his knife and fork. His eyes had a distant look. "She must miss Joel terribly."

Kyle nodded. She could see how deeply Kenneth sensed the loss. The thought of Joel's death made her own heart constrict.

"I'm sure, beyond her longing for Joel," Kenneth went on, "it must be hard for a single mother to care for the needs of herself and her child. And Ruthie does not have any secure income. She's dependent on what comes in at the mission."

"Charity," Kyle murmured.

"Exactly," Kenneth agreed, without any acknowledgment of her tone. "At least in a way."

Kyle kept her voice casual. "Why doesn't she give up the mission work and just go back home? I'm sure she'd be welcomed with open arms."

"She certainly would. Simon was at the mission today as well. He said they don't want to insist, but they've tried and tried to get her back to the farm."

"Why doesn't she, then?"

Kenneth's eyes widened in surprise, as though he would have expected her to know the answer for herself. "She's there because the ministry of Morning Glory meant so much to Joel. And to her. And all her recent memories of her husband—"

"But surely her son means more!"

Kenneth looked taken aback by her vehemence. He rested his elbows on the table as he looked at Kyle. "Of course he does."

"Then why doesn't she consider him first?"

Kenneth's powerful gaze was focused fully upon her now. "I'm sure she does. But the mission work was Joel's dream. His life. If Ruthie deserted it, I imagine she'd feel as though she was deserting him and his memory as well. Can you see that?"

But Kyle was unable to respond. It felt as if a thousand shreds of thoughts were suddenly spinning through her mind, tugging at her heart, whispering ideas into her head that she could scarcely hear, much less believe that she was even considering.

"Kyle, darling, it's dreadfully hard to find people who are willing to commit time and love to helping those on the streets. Ruthie loves these poor lost ones. Not just be-cause of Joel either. It's her own calling as well. She feels the mission is where God wants her to serve. She has said time and time again that God will provide for her and the baby. She feels confident of that." Kenneth's gaze probed deeply. "You understand that, don't you?" When Kyle did not answer, he said, "I believe God has a solution for Ruthie and her baby that includes the mission. I think we should pray that the Lord will clearly show that to her. In the meantime, we can give a bit more this month to help with her support."

Kyle rose to her feet and began collecting their dinner plates. She did not want to sit there under his gaze any longer. The battle within her was too powerful, too telling. There had been a time when she had trusted God, too. Trusted Him to heal her baby. But He hadn't. He had let her down. She feared that He might let Ruthie down as well. Ruthie and the beautiful baby boy that was her broth-er's child.

For long into the night Kyle lay awake. The dark hours held a strangeness, for she seemed to be listening to only one part of what her mind and her heart were saying. She struggled not to hear the other whispers, the ones further down inside her. And in her confusion and unrest she ig-nored entirely Kenneth's admonition to pray. She struggled with the problem, working it this way and that, seeking her own solution.

Near morning it hit her with the force of a blow. Why had it taken her so long to think of it? She had a perfectly reasonable answer. With the idea's arrival, the longing in her heart focused and tightened until she ached with something like hunger. But she tried not to think about that.

Kyle felt tension and excitement and relief all surge through her, everything so tangled together that she was able to ignore everything except what she wanted to hear. Her solution was perfectly feasible, and Ruthie would be free to continue the work of their beloved mission.

CHAPTER TWENTY-ONE

ALTHOUGH HINTS OF SPRING finally arrived with that last week in April, temperatures remained far below normal. Many nights still touched freezing, giving Ruthie nightmares as she thought of the young people who did not have shelter. All that winter they had brought in as many as they could find. But even now, with spring at least indicated on the mission's kitchen calendar, it meant the place was bulging at the seams. She dared not think about what the fire marshal might say.

A slight shift in the buzz of conversation caught Ruthie's attention. She rose from her desk and started moving toward the person silhouetted in the doorway before she had fully worked out who it was. Then the light shifted, and her smile captured her whole face.

"Kyle, how wonderful!" She walked straight up and hugged her. Ruthie ignored the resistance she could feel through the elegant ankle-length coat. She might not be used to embracing people dressed in such finery, but Ruthie made it her practice to hug others, no matter what their station in life. Many of the young people here were frightened by touch. She ignored their fears because hugging

155

them was a way of making them feel welcome, letting them know that what was offered here was more than just a roof and a meal. When they relaxed, as Kyle seemed to be doing now, Ruthie felt as though she had won a battle for her Lord.

She held Kyle at arm's length. "I'm so glad to see you. You look terrific." Which was true, so long as she did not look too closely into those empty eyes. "How are you?"

"I should be asking you that," Kyle said, her smile twisting slightly to one side.

"Oh, I'm so busy these days it's almost possible to forget the pain," Ruth returned warmly. "And then I'm too tired not to sleep." For some reason her words unsettled Kyle, she could tell; so Ruthie slipped one arm through Kyle's and drew her forward. "Come, let's go into the chapel. It's the one quiet place these days."

They picked their way around several clusters of young people, some on threadbare sofas and others on the floor. Here and there guitars were strumming, the chords and songs forming a cacophony of sound. Kyle asked, "What are they singing?"

"Mostly protest songs about one thing or another. It's the fashion these days."

"Doesn't the noise bother you?"

"Not enough that I would complain. I need to be needed." She led her guest into the little corner chapel, really just a room off the main chamber and furnished with a small podium, a cross on the wall, and folding chairs. Ruthie waited until they were seated to repeat, "How are you, Kyle?"

"Fine. I'm fine."

"We've missed seeing you around here. I have missed you. And little Samuel—"

"That's actually what I wanted to talk to you about."

Kyle pulled a handkerchief from her coat pocket and began twisting it between her fingers. "The baby, I mean."

The way Kyle tightened the handkerchief made Ruthie think she often went through these motions. "What about him, what about Samuel?"

"You must be so busy these days here at the mission. All by yourself, I mean."

"I have thought about going back to the farm," Ruthie acknowledged. "But it wouldn't be possible to leave all that Joel has made. This is his legacy. I feel so close to him here." Ruthie found herself watching Kyle's hands and the handkerchief. "I do go up to the farm often. I'm going tomorrow, as a matter of fact, so it's good that you came—"

"I wasn't talking about the farm," Kyle said, her voice as tight as the handkerchief. "I was talking about . . . about Samuel. Your baby."

"What about him?" Ruthie's voice held her bewilderment.

"I have a proposal, a solution to your problem," Kyle said in a rush. "An idea that would help both of you. You would be free to continue Joel's work here without any worries about the baby, and little Samuel would be raised—"

"What?" Ruthie had to fight to catch a breath.

"He would be raised with every advantage," Kyle hurried on. "And he has the same family bloodlines as I do. . . ." Her voice drifted to a stop.

Ruth struggled to speak above the turmoil in her heart. "Kyle—"

"I know you want the best for Samuel, and you can't possibly give the baby a proper upbringing alone. Kyle pressed on. "Especially here. Think of the danger of disease, and you hardly have enough to live on. But if he were with me . . ."

Ruthie forced her legs to straighten and drew herself upright. "If you mean—mean give up Samuel, you must know I could never do that." She paused and looked directly into Kyle's face. "I don't think I understand. . . . I really must be going."

Kyle seemed to take no notice of Ruthie's horrified response. She released the handkerchief long enough to hold out her hand toward Ruthie. "Please, Ruthie, give it some thought before you say no," she said as her sister-in-law shrank from her touch. "Think of everything I could give him."

CHAPTER TWENTY-TWO

THE STORM OF FEELINGS accompanied Ruthie on her trip up to the Miller farm. They darkened the entire journey, isolating her from all but the baby in her arms. Every now and then she felt a rush of panic that there might indeed be a certain logic behind what Kyle had proposed. Then she tightened her embrace of Samuel and the horror rose fresh and strong, leaving her feeling ill to her stomach.

The only reason she ate at all that evening was because the baby needed nourishment. Her family, lovingly conscious of her mood, let her be. After all, she had lost her husband only a few months before.

She rose before the sun, glad to return to the farm's simple routines and early morning chores. In spite of her distress, she saw the mark of hard times everywhere she went. There were fewer animals, and those still around bore the lean, hungry look of beasts at the end of a long winter.

The family watched her in their quiet way, waiting until she was ready to speak for herself. Ruthie was not sure she should say anything about her traumatic encounter with Kyle. But after an inner debate she decided she had to tell someone, and who better than her family to help her sort it all out?

She waited until after breakfast. Mornings were a good time for sharing secrets. The sun had not yet warmed the earth, and fewer chores clamored for attention than in the summertime. Once the breakfast dishes were washed and put away, the family returned to the big breakfast table for their Bible reading and prayer. And she told them what Kyle had said.

She held nothing back. Not even the doubts that had come to her in the night, the ones which whispered that perhaps Kyle was right. Perhaps she should give the baby to Kyle and let him enjoy all the things she could not give him. Speaking in the Old German tongue helped Ruthie distance herself from the life in Washington and all her worries. It gave her the ability to stand away and observe her situation from a fresh perspective.

When she finished, she felt drained but satisfied. She knew that baby Samuel would stay with her. The doubts that had plagued her the night after Kyle's visit had no place here in this home. The baby was hers—hers and Joel's. Samuel would be raised with all the love and care she could give him.

To her surprise, it was not her father who spoke first. Instead, just as Joseph opened his mouth, Simon rose to his feet, moving so swiftly that his chair clattered over behind him.

"Everybody wait right here," he demanded. "I have something to tell you." He turned to Sarah, his younger sister, a grave expression in his eyes. "Unless you object."

She started to speak but stopped and bit her lip. She glanced at Ruthie, then gave her head a shake. No. She did not mind.

Simon left the room. Ruthie's mother turned to her

husband with a troubled expression, but before she could voice the question in her eyes, Joseph raised one hand. Wait.

Simon soon came back, bearing a worn and tattered leather wallet. He pushed it across the table to his father and declared, "This is for Ruthie."

Joseph picked up the wallet and looked in astonishment at the bills stacked inside. "What is this?"

"Papa, Patience and I, we want to wed." His voice trembled with the effort of speaking. "The Brueders are . . . are as hard up as we. All winter we have worked, saving up a dowry."

"I helped, Papa," Sarah added. "It was fun."

"My tool shed," their mother cried. "And all those hours you spent at the markets. I knew it was taking you too long to sell so few eggs."

Joseph had not touched the money. He looked from the wallet to his son and back again. "What have you done for this money?"

"We dried flowers, Papa. Wild flowers we gathered last autumn. We didn't want to say anything because we weren't sure . . ." He had to stop for a breath. "It was Patience's idea. She heard about it from one of the stores. Sarah made the bouquets with her."

Joseph stared at him. "So much they pay for dead flowers?"

"Eight hundred and seventeen dollars, Papa. We wanted to use it for planting some acres of flowers this summer. Then maybe in the fall we have our wedding." He turned to look at Ruthie. "But I want you to have it. You need it. For the baby."

Ruthie had to swallow the sudden lump in her throat before she could speak. "Simon, I can't take your dowry."

"Yes you can. You must. Samuel is your son, Ruthie.

161

He is *yours*." He crossed his arms determinedly, showing the strength in his body and his spirit. "I know Patience will agree. The money is yours."

A shaky breath from the head of the table brought them all around. Joseph's beard trembled as he struggled for control. He raised a work-worn hand and wiped at the corners of his eyes. Finally he managed, "Such a family I have been given. Such riches." He looked at his son with shining eyes. "This day you have made me very proud."

Simon blushed under the praise. "It wasn't just me, Papa. Sarah is an artist. You should see what she can do with the flowers. And Patience, she—"

"I was not speaking of the flowers. The flowers can wait for another talk." He gestured at the wallet on the table before him. "I am speaking of your gift. For you and Patience to offer your sister the dowry your own fathers cannot give . . ."

Joseph Miller stopped and covered his eyes with one hand. He sat there for a long moment, utterly still, while they all held their breath.

As they sat and waited, the sun cleared the roof of the barn. Light streamed through the back window and splashed joyfully upon the table. The sudden light brought a sheen of tears to Ruthie's eyes.

Joseph dropped his hand and said to his son, "Make your wedding plans. I will be speaking to Papa Brueder. Save this money for your planting."

"But, Papa—"

"Enough, I tell you, enough." He turned and looked at Ruthie. "You know what you are to do."

"Yes, Papa," she said softly. "The baby is mine."

"Have Kyle come to see me, if she will. It is time for

us to talk. She needs help to heal these wounds." He bent for his crutch, then pushed himself erect. He turned and looked once more at his son and murmured, "The richest man in all the world."

CHAPTER TWENTY-THREE

TO THE CASUAL OBSERVER, Abigail was a picture of brisk and competent composure. She kept up an energetic pace down the Washington street, her chin high, her gaze level. But inwardly she was uncomfortable and ill at ease.

Her interior confusion had nothing to do with the undefined physical malaise that had nagged at her for several weeks now. The day before, Abigail had stopped by Kyle's home. Kyle had made a polite query over her health, and then she launched into a long description of a charity concert Abigail had missed.

Abigail sat there listening to her daughter and glancing around the room. She had never seen it so tidy—not one item out of place. Cut flowers stood in a vase at the center of the coffee table. Every surface was shining, and the air smelled of polish and cleaner. Every piece of furniture and china was exactly in its place. Even the clock on the mantel seemed to tick with proper exactness.

Her attention returned to Kyle, who had chatted on about the women who had attended the function, the food that was served, the decorations in the room. She made little asides about the outfits a couple of them were wearing. Now when Abigail thought back over the visit, she realized there was not a single instant of silence the entire hour that she was with Kyle.

Abigail continued walking down the Washington street, knowing exactly why the experience at Kyle's had made her feel so uneasy. She stared idly into one beautifully presented showroom window after another, but in truth she saw very little. Despite the veneer of normalcy, despite her daughter's animation, Abigail had understood exactly why she herself had remained so concerned. It was the same thing which she had confronted that first time Kyle and Kenneth had joined her for church. The same thing she had noticed in her daughter numerous times since then. With every passing day, Kyle was becoming more and more like herself.

The day before, she had sat and listened to Kyle parrot all the perspectives she was coming to dislike most in herself. Her daughter's empty words had been grating, both because they pointed at what Kyle was becoming, and because they showed how helpless Abigail was in the face of what she had come to see as wrong, both with herself and with her daughter.

Abigail stopped so suddenly the woman walking behind her brushed against her with a startled apology. But Abigail paid no notice. Her attention was held by the reflection in the window. Abigail stood and stared back at herself, and realized what troubled her even more today. She had never felt so helpless. She knew what the problem was, yet had no idea what the solution could be. It felt as though all the years of mistakes and false pretenses were there in front of her eyes, forcing her to realize just what an enormous error she had made of raising her own child.

All those years of pushing and prodding the child because she was not the proper young lady Abigail desired and demanded—the weight of it suddenly seemed unbearable. She looked in the mirrorlike surface of the window and saw the hollowness underneath her perfect exterior. And she saw Kyle.

If only there was something she could do. Some way to correct all the errors. Some way to make everything better. For herself, and for her daughter.

Kyle felt sluggish and headachy. She had made a feeble attempt at morning prayer and had finally gotten dressed, her thoughts distracted and her soul unsatisfied. Inwardly she told herself that she would pray later when her mind was more at rest. But she knew she wouldn't. She had made that empty promise on many other days.

She had not slept well. The night before she had tried to reach Ruthie, only to learn that she was still up at the Miller farm. Kyle could not understand what was taking her so long to respond. Every minute seemed to drag as she waited for Ruthie to answer.

Kyle wandered aimlessly to the kitchen. Perhaps a cup of coffee would help. Without conscious thought she measured the coffee, added the water, and placed the pot on the electric burner. She wasn't sure she wanted coffee at all. Wasn't sure she wanted anything. Perhaps she should go out. Maybe call Abigail. No, Abigail would see her dark-rimmed eyes and probably ask questions. Martha? No. Martha would look at her with all that love and pain in her face. Kyle was in no mood to handle Martha's loving sympathy. Shopping? Merely the thought of meandering through the stores made her feel worse. Impatiently she snatched open the cupboard and stared unseeing at the array of cups.

She needed to get out. Away. Somewhere. To fill her mind with some kind of coherent activity. Some purpose for making it through another day.

The coffee began to send out its rich aroma, but Kyle hardly noticed as she automatically selected a cup. Her scattered thoughts were interrupted by the ringing of the doorbell. Kyle frowned. Who was ringing at this hour of the morning?

She had taken a few steps toward the front door before her mind registered a faint sound . . . almost like a little whimper. She found herself hurrying across the front hallway, drawn by what she did not understand.

She opened the door to Abigail. "Mother! Have I forgotten something? An appointment?"

"No, no . . ." Abigail seemed strangely uncomfortable. "I, well, that is . . ."

"Come in." In fact, Kyle found herself glad that her mother had stopped by. Since Abigail was walking in unannounced, she would find some excuse for her drawn features. Everybody had bad nights now and then. "I just made some fresh coffee."

"Kyle . . ." Abigail hesitated on the little front porch. "I was walking by a shop this morning, and I found myself, well, thinking of how much you always wanted a pet."

"Excuse me?"

"I don't know how to say this." Abigail seemed to search the air above her head. "Oh, I don't even know what it is I want to say."

"Mother—" There it was again. The faintest of sounds, a little scratching and a high-pitched whimper.

"Kyle, I wasn't always the best mother to you. I know that. We both do." Abigail's words pushed against one another, as though she had spent the entire journey trying to decide what to say. "But I did what I thought was best at the time."

"Of course you did," Kyle said, trying to peer behind Abigail.

"But now, well, I wish I had done some things differently." Abigail stopped a moment, then managed, "And I was thinking that perhaps—that is, I was recalling how much you wanted a puppy when you were young."

Finally it dawned on Kyle. "You bought me a dog?"

"I was just passing by the store this morning and there it was in the window. The shopkeeper told me it was the runt of the litter. All the others had long since been bought, and they had put this last one up front so at least it could have the passersby for company."

Kyle held her breath as Abigail spoke. Yes, she had always wanted a dog as a child. But she was an adult now. An adult whose home should be filled with the laughter of a growing child instead of the emptiness that echoed and followed her from room to room. She started to protest. Surely Abigail did not think that a dog, any dog, could fill the void in her life. Surely not.

Abigail seemed to read her thoughts. "I know you've been so lonely. And hurt. And I thought this little dog looked lonely too. Perhaps, well, I just thought the two of you might help each other." The last sentence came out in a rush.

Kyle felt her sudden irritation melt away. This was so unlike her mother. The words, the thoughts, the effort. It was hard to be upset with her just now. "Where is he?"

"She. It's a little female. She's, well . . ." Abigail made a vague gesture behind her. "In that small carrier out by the walk."

Then Kyle spotted the little screened box and thought she saw a movement inside. She hastened down the steps and along the walk. The tiny whine was clearly heard now.

Abigail followed along behind her. "She's been all alone in the pen since the beginning of last week. That seemed like such a long time, well . . ."

Kyle bent over the box and lifted the peaked lid. A pair of soulful dark eyes surrounded by soft golden curls stared up at her. "It's a spaniel."

"Pure-bred cocker." Abigail stooped beside her daughter. "Quite a pretty dog."

Kyle was unprepared for the sudden lurch of her heart. It seemed to reach out even before her hand as she moved to stroke the soft curls. "Poor little thing."

It turned brown pleading eyes toward her and a small pink tongue licked tentatively at her fingers. Kyle lifted the little animal. "She's beautiful, Mother."

Abigail opened her mouth, clearly wanting to say something more, but words did not come. She reached one hand out toward Kyle but ended up simply stroking the puppy's little head. Then she said, "I really must be going. The entire day is off schedule now." But her attempt at a brisk tone did not cover the softness and concern in her face.

Kyle's heart went out to her mother. She felt an unbidden surge of tears as confusing emotions and images tried to force their way out. Kyle could only manage a nod. Just a small tip of her head, but it must have been enough for Abigail. She gave a nod of her own, and with a sad smile turned to make her way back up the street.

Kyle stood and watched her disappear around the corner. Later she would need to find some way to thank Abigail. But not just now. She buried her face in the softness of the puppy's fur and heard the soft whine in response.

CHAPTER TWENTY-FOUR

KYLE WAS REACHING FOR her coat when the phone rang. She lifted the receiver to her mother's "Good morning, dear. How are you today?"

"Hello, Mother. I'm in a rush." Kyle picked up the phone cradle, pulled the cord free, and walked over to glance through the narrow side window. The street was empty. "I've ordered a taxi."

"This early?"

"I'm going up to the Miller farm." Finally, finally, the call had come through from Ruthie.

"Isn't Kenneth in New York for that big meeting?"

"Yes. He left last night. I'm going alone." She did not bother to say she had organized her own trip to coincide with Kenneth's absence.

"Does he know you're going to the Millers'?"

"Of course, Mother." There was no need to relate the questions she had been forced to avoid answering. "I'll be back tomorrow before he comes in."

"Well, would you like me to—" But she stopped before she finished making the offer. Clearly Abigail could not imagine herself at the Miller farm—or any farm, for that matter.

"I'll be fine, Mother. I need to . . . to see Ruthie," she finished vaguely.

Her phone conversation with Ruthie had been confusing. At first the girl had seemed so definite that, no, she was not going to give up the baby. But then Ruthie had said Mr. Miller wanted to see her. Kyle had felt a stab of hope. What other reason could there be for such a meeting, except that he wanted to talk to her about taking the baby? So there had to be a chance after all. But this was nothing she could explain to either Kenneth or to Abigail. They would hear about it only when all was definite and final.

Abigail sighed, "Oh. I see. Very well."

Another glance through the front window. Still no taxi. "Why did you call?"

"Oh, it's nothing, really. I had a favor to ask." Abigail stopped, and Kyle waited for her to explain. "I went in the other day for a physical. The doctor's office called last night." Another breath. "The doctor in charge of my examination wants me to come in to see him this morning."

The news drew Kyle away from the window. "Is something wrong?"

"I'm sure I don't know. I haven't really been feeling like myself, but . . ." Another pause, then, "I was hoping you could come with me."

"Anytime but today, Mother." Which was not exactly true. Kyle was not sure she would be able to force herself into another medical facility anytime soon. "The Millers have invited me up, and it's important."

"Well, if you're sure." Kyle said nothing in response. Abigail took a breath and said, "How's your puppy?"

"Oh, Goldie's fine. She's asleep in the kitchen. A neighbor agreed to stop in and check on her this afternoon and again tonight."

"You've named the dog Goldie?"

"Kenneth says it's not a very imaginative name, but I think it suits her. Her coat just shines with the brushing and bath."

Abigail's tone warmed. "I'm glad you're making her part of the family."

"Yes, we are." Family. Kyle glanced through the window again. The street remained empty. "Kenneth says Goldie is becoming a one-woman dog. Her eyes do seem to follow me everywhere I go. And all I need to do is sit down for a moment and she's right there beside me."

"I wish I had let you have one when you were young," Abigail confessed. "I wish . . ."

"What?"

"Oh, nothing. What's done is done." But she sounded very sad.

Kyle decided it had to be the doctor's appointment that was worrying her mother. She paced back to the hall table and put the phone set down. "They probably just want to run a few tests," she said with as much confidence as she could. "I'll call you as soon as I get to the train station."

"I won't be back by then. And they've already run more tests than I thought existed." Abigail tried for briskness. "It's probably nothing. Call me when you get home."

"Yes. Of course I will." She started to turn back to the window, but her attention was snagged by her reflection in the tall oval mirror.

"Have a good trip, dear. And do take care."

"Thank you, Mother." Kyle slowly hung up the phone without glancing away from her reflection. She was dressed in a new dark blue two-piece outfit she had bought with her mother. A lady's suit, the saleswoman had called it, enthusing over how lovely the designer ensemble had looked on Kyle's slender frame. And she did look good. In fact, she probably had never looked better. Her hair was precisely cut in a fashionable style, her makeup as perfect as she could do it. A silk blouse of palest gray, a single strand of pearls, matching earrings, and pumps and purse the exact shade of her suit completed the look.

But it was not her comely appearance that held her so. It was the expression on her face, in her eyes, as she had finished speaking with her mother. Kyle lifted her hand from the receiver and touched her cheek.

Her eyes were what held her. Not the tension in her features, nor the firm way her mouth was pursed, nor the narrow lines etched across her forehead. Her eyes.

A sudden thought struck her. She had seen that gaze before. The eyes had been a different color, but the gaze had been the same. The same tightness, the same emptiness. They had stared down at her throughout her childhood years, checking her appearance, her behavior, disapproving of everything she had done and was. Kyle stood and looked at her face and wondered when she had taken on Abigail's gaze. And where her own eyes had gone.

A horn honked, startling Kyle. She rushed to open the door, wave to the taxi, then went back to retrieve her purse and case. Kyle forced herself to avoid her reflection in the mirror as she turned and walked from the house.

Abigail had always prided herself on knowing how to be prepared for anything. Today she had three magazines, the newspaper, and a book she had heard discussed by a news commentator. But the paper remained folded on the chair beside her, and the magazines lay unopened on her lap.

She looked around the half-empty waiting room. They all smelled the same, these places. No matter how well appointed the room was, or how nice and attractive the receptionist might be, or what pretty art they put on the walls, it was still a doctor's office. They all smelled vaguely of antiseptic and fear. Pain and uncertainty seemed to have seeped into the walls and the furniture, adding to the concern she already felt about the doctor's summons.

A woman came through the door leading from the examining rooms. She had been crying. Her makeup had been cleaned away, but Abigail could still see a smudge on either cheek, and her eyes were red. Abigail knew she should not be staring, but she could not help herself. It was like looking through a window into her own future.

The receptionist gave the woman a smile of forced cheeriness and handed over a slip. "We've set up the appointment for you tomorrow morning at nine. Here, see, I've written down the room you need to report to at the hospital. Now be sure not to eat or drink anything after dinner tonight, all right?"

The woman accepted the paper without looking at it or the receptionist. She turned and started for the door. Abigail sat and watched until the woman had left. Only then could she manage to draw a full breath.

"Mrs. Rothmore?" The receptionist turned her professional smile in Abigail's direction. "Good morning. The doctor is ready to see you now."

Abigail gathered her magazine and newspaper, trying to force her hands to stop their trembling. She rose unsteadily to her feet, not even making an attempt to respond to the nurse's greeting. She followed the woman down the long hallway and was directed into a small room. The doctor was not there. Abigail sank into a chair and stared at nothing as the nurse closed the door, leaving her alone. A file with her name was lying there on the desk. She had no desire to take a look.

There in the empty, lonely room, she felt something she had never known before. Not as a child when her father had lost the family fortune, not when her husband's new company teetered on the brink of disaster, not when she learned she could not have children, not when her husband died, never once. Until now. Abigail did not just feel lonely and frightened. She felt defeated.

Here and now, her life had been taken out of her control. There was nothing she could do about what she faced. The inevitability left her bereft and stripped of her defenses. All those little white lies—and the big black ones. Now they all came crashing down around her. Every last one. It felt as though the structure of her entire life, all her protection, was crumbling around her, turning to the dust that she would soon become.

The door opened. The doctor entered and said briskly, "Good morning, Mrs. Rothmore. How are you today?"

But Abigail could not have responded even if she had wanted to. She was weeping far too hard to speak a single word.

CHAPTER TWENTY-FIVE

THE MILLERS HAD HELD LUNCH for her arrival. It was the most difficult meal Kyle had ever eaten, but not for the reason she would have expected. She was nervous, yes, and eager to sit down and speak with Mr. Miller. The entire train ride she had tried to concentrate on all the points she would make. How she could give the baby a good home. How she would make plans for him to get into the proper kindergarten and then the best private school in the nation. How he would lack for nothing. Of course, that was why Mr. Miller had asked to see her. He could see how important it was, and he would talk to Ruthie.

But the lunch was unsettling. The family was very friendly to her. She had expected to find some resistance, possibly even some hostility. After all, she was clearly so much better off than they were. She could see the effects of their hardship everywhere. The house and the outbuildings all desperately needed painting. The Miller family's clothing was worn and mended. The farmyard was strangely silent, as though there weren't many animals around. And the simple food on the table fed them all, but there were no offers of seconds.

And yet they were all so *happy*. The talk was cheerful, their greetings warm. They asked about everything—her life, her family, her husband. The only subject they did not mention was Ruthie and the child. She tried to bring it up on several occasions, but it was just brushed aside. Finally Kyle accepted that she would have to wait. But the lunch and the questions seemed to go on forever. She felt unsettled by their genuine interest in her. These kind people and their gentle questions seemed to pry at the seal she had set in place over her heart.

Time after time she found herself thinking back to the image she had seen in the mirror that morning. These people could not have been kinder, more caring, more thoughtful and concerned. Why did she keep remembering how she had looked, and the expression she had seen in her own eyes? Why did she feel so threatened? Was she afraid that she would not be able to keep everything in place, that they might expose what she was carefully keeping hidden inside?

After lunch Mr. Miller invited her to join him on the porch. Her heart hammered in her chest as she walked slowly behind the big graying man. His crutch thumped and the floor creaked as he crossed to the oversized padded chair in the porch's far corner. He smiled up at her. "Sit down, my child. Why do you stand?"

"Oh. I . . . thank you."

"Choel, he made this seat for me with his own hands. And Ruthie, she sewed the cushions." Joseph Miller beamed. "Such riches a man has, with a family like mine."

That was her opening. Kyle leaned forward and said, "Thank you so much for seeing me today, Mr. Miller."

"Ach, what is this Mr. Miller? I am Choseph to you. Still are we family. And always will we count you as one of us."

"Thank you . . . Joseph. Actually, I wanted—"

"Patience is needed in speaking with the old," Joseph said gently, the light in his eyes inviting her to calm down. "Something is needed to be spoken. Good it is that you are here. You will now give me patience and hear my words?"

"Of course," Kyle said, forcing herself to settle back. She would wait. She had no choice.

"Sister of Choel, listen carefully. God is a good God. He is always faithful and chust. This means He does everything right, and He does everything in the right way. Yah, yah, I know. You have your reasons to think other thoughts. But these words, still they are true. Maybe there is blessing for one and suffering for another. Maybe life is hard, and we wonder, where is our God? Maybe even we think, how God has let this happen? Why does it happen again today? When will there be an answer to my need?"

A sermon. Just what she needed. Kyle tried to feel irritation, impatience. But instead, she felt frightened. Exposed. Somehow the words shook her as nothing had in, well, months and months. The tone was gentle. Joseph did not even look at her most of the time. Yet the power of his kindhearted talk reached deep into her and began to pry away her fiercely guarded barriers.

"I am a simple man. Reasons are not here for why we must suffer. I cannot explain the sadness of life. No. All I can say is that always will God be with us. Always. Yah, this I *know*. In the darkness, in the suffering. So long as we let Him into our hearts and receive His comfort. For receive it we must. Like a gift. I hold it out to you but you must take it."

He demonstrated with his hand toward her, then he reached up and began to stroke the long gray beard. She found herself staring at the hand, unable to turn away. It was creased and hardened and scarred, that hand. The fingernails were stained and battered by years and years of hard work. But the action seemed so gentle, so thoughtful, just like the words.

"I sit here and I think. It is an old man's way, to think on things. I think, yah, my life has been hard. It has cost much, this life. I think about the days before, and sometimes a glimmer comes. A tiny ray, like the sun just rising on a summer day. I think of Peter, the apostle who stumbled like me. Once he turns to the Lord and asks about his end. The Lord tells him because Peter, he is the Lord's friend. A simple man with many faults, yah, but still a friend. So Peter, he points to another man and says, What about this man here, how will his end be? And you know what the Lord says? You know this part of your Bible?"

Kyle realized with a pang of guilt that she had not opened her Bible for many days. And how much longer had it been since she had really absorbed the words? Kyle licked dry lips. "No," she acknowledged.

"Ach, it is a small passage. But spoke to me it did, that passage. I ask that so often, you know. Why me and not that man? I ask. But the Lord, He said to Peter, If this is what I will, what is that to you? The Lord, He was saying, think you only of your own fate, not that of another. Think you of your own faith. Think you of your own salvation. Think of God's purpose for you."

The chair creaked as Joseph Miller shifted to draw it closer to her. His eyes glowed as he looked at her, seeming to examine far below the surface, deep into the areas that she had tried so hard to hide away forever. "So careful must we be, careful always when we look at the victories and the defeats of life. Careful to hold room for the *mystery* of God. The power of our Lord to turn defeat and pain and suffering into good—He is good for each of us."

She wanted to come back with something bitter. Something drawn from the well that he was exposing, the pain and the distress and the unwanted memories. But she could not speak. For there alongside all the agony was something else. A peace and a healing touch so gentle she could not fight it. Could not force it away, even as it threatened her efforts to hold everything in place.

Joseph Miller seemed to understand her turmoil. He nodded slowly, his gaze piercing now, the light in them almost blinding. But his voice remained gentle as he quietly said, "You are angry with God that He took your baby." She opened her mouth to protest, but he said, "You think God makes a mistake. But you do not want to say that, even to yourself. So, instead, you hide your heart away, far away from your family who loves you. And you hide your heart away from God."

Kyle's eyes dropped to her hands twisting in her lap. But his voice compelled her to look at him again as he said, "When we face failure in our life, hold we must to God. When we weep, it is on God's shoulder that we cry. When we suffer, it is with Him there beside us. Why? Because then will He *heal* us. Then will He *make whole again*.

"And when life pushes and tugs and tries to pull us away from God, this must we remember: The symbol of our King is the Cross. The Father lost His Son, too. Lost to separate us from our sins, the whole world's sin. Lost to death, He was. Tragic, painful death." He waited a long moment, his gaze reaching as deep as his words, then finished quietly, "The Lord God, our Father knows, my daughter. He *knows*."

CHAPTER TWENTY-SIX

KYLE HURRIED UP THE long drive to the Rothmore estate, her face set by the panic she had heard in Abigail's voice. She did not want to be here at all, and most especially she did not want to be here today. Even so, she could not have denied Abigail's plea that she come out. She had never heard the woman's voice so—what? So broken. On top of her visit to the Millers' farm, Kyle felt as though her own world was being shaken to its very core.

When the large stone mansion came into view, she had a moment's pang over all the past and all the memories. It had been over a year since her last visit to her childhood home. Kyle climbed the stairs, relieved that the faces from her childhood were not there with expressions of their concern. Old Jim, the former gardener, now had a small apartment in Baltimore near his daughter. Maggie and Bertrand, the housekeepers, had retired to the Maryland coast. Even so, they all seemed very close just then, and Kyle felt a twinge at the thought of all of Maggie's unopened letters gathering dust in her top drawer. She had felt she just couldn't face the truth they would contain.

Kyle unlocked the door and pushed it open. The maid

who had been with her through those first dark weeks came rushing up. "Miss Kyle, thank the good Lord you've come."

"Where's Mother?"

"She's upstairs, Miss Kyle, and she's fit to be tied."

Evelyn. That was the woman's name. Kyle felt yet another twinge over the way she had treated her. Kyle tried to shake it off as she headed for the stairway, but the feeling of guilt following her could not be dispatched so easily. Kyle ran up the stairs and down the long upstairs hall, stopping outside her mother's door. She had a fleeting impression of another door, one hidden deep within herself, that gradually was being cracked open, and the first whispers were emerging.

She shook her head against the thought, knocked on the door, and called, "Mother?"

"Oh, Kyle. Thank goodness." There was the sound of footsteps hurrying across the floor, then the door flew back, and a woman she knew but did not know pulled her into a frantic embrace. "I've been so afraid and so alone."

Kyle could not keep the panic from her own voice. "Tell me what's the matter!"

Abigail grasped her hand tightly, pulled her inside, pushed the door closed, and led her across to the chairs by the window. "I went to the doctor's yesterday."

"What did he say? Tell me!"

"Nothing." Abigail almost fell into her chair, picked the crumpled hankie off the narrow table, and waved it in the air. "That's not important."

"Mother, it most certainly is!" Kyle remained standing, fighting off the urge to take her mother's shoulders and shake them. "Tell me what he said!"

"He said it's nothing—I'm fine." But instead of looking pleased, fresh tears seeped out from the corners of Abigail's eyes. "Don't you understand? I'm fine *now*."

"No." All the strength in Kyle's body drained away. If the chair had not been right there, she might have fallen to the floor. Kyle slumped down into the seat. "No, Mother. I don't understand at all."

"There was a woman leaving as I arrived." Abigail's distracted manner was most unusual and out of character. Kyle searched her face as Abigail continued. "That's what started me off, I suppose. Or maybe it was the look in Kenneth's eyes that day at church, or something from our conversation. . . . Oh, I don't know. It doesn't matter. I saw that woman at the doctor's office, Kyle, and it was devastating. She was looking death straight in the face. And right then I knew."

Kyle felt more than confusion. She felt as though every carefully constructed wall of defense, everything which had seen her through the past months, was crumbling. She did not know why seeing her mother so distressed would have that effect on her. But it did. "Knew what, Mother?" she begged.

"That I'm not ready to die." The words ripped away what control Abigail had left. "No matter that it's not coming today or tomorrow. Then and there I knew it was *coming*, and I'm not *ready*." She buried her face in her hands, and the muffled words emerged, "All my life has been a lie."

"Mother, I'm not . . . you're . . ."

Abigail lifted her tear-streaked face. "Oh, Kyle, I've been so awful to you and to everyone. I've manipulated and I've schemed and I've demanded until I'm blue in the face. I've never had any true friends. Even when I started going to church, it was all a lie. I knew if I didn't go, I'd risk losing you. But I never really gave my heart to God. I suppose I never understood that until the moment in the doctor's office when I saw just how alone I truly was. Alone in this life, and alone in the next. No friends, Kyle. And what I do have is this terrible emptiness inside. . . ."

Kyle started at the familiar-sounding description coming from Abigail. With great effort, she reached across the chasm separating them and placed one hand upon Abigail's arm. "You have me, Mother. I'm your friend."

"I know I don't deserve you. Not after everything . . ." Abigail had difficulty forcing the words around her sobs. "But I had to call, you see. You are the only one who can help me."

The air seemed to compress around her, forming a myriad of gentle hands reaching down to brush aside all the remaining defenses. All the wounds and fears and longings and pains, all exposed and naked to the light of day. Kyle worked her mouth, but no sound came out. She swallowed and managed to whisper, "Help you how, Mother?"

"Learn how to pray." One hand scrunched the hankie to her temple, while the other reached up to grasp Kyle's arm. "Do you think it's too late? Do you think God still wants me?"

CHAPTER TWENTY-SEVEN

ONCE AGAIN KYLE STOPPED in her front hallway to inspect the street through the narrow window. She did not yet see Kenneth. From the kitchen there came the sound of a puppy's whimper, but Kyle could not take the time to see to her dog just then. She paced back into the living room and glanced at the clock over the mantel. What could be keeping him, today of all days?

The clock's ticking followed her back into the front hall, the sound a constant, steady reminder of all that had come before—all the isolation, all the mistakes, all the selfishness. Her path took her in front of the mirror where she was confronted with her own reflection. She tried not to look, but she could not help the single glance which revealed the frantic features, the desperate eyes. Yes. That was what she had been hiding all along. Desperation. Despair and helplessness and fear and pain. And she had been hiding from God's love.

From outside came the sound of a car door slamming. Kyle ran to open the front door and flew down the steps, rushing into Kenneth's arms. He caught her in a strong embrace. "Kyle, honey, what's the matter?"

"Oh, Kenneth," she said, and then the sobs of a year of holding back came pouring out. "I'm so afraid. I've been so wrong."

"Sweetheart, darling, come on, let's go inside." Gently he steered her around and brought her up the stairs and back inside the house. He closed the door behind them, then wrapped both arms around his wife. "Tell me."

"Oh, it's so confusing. I don't even know where to start."

"Try."

So she started with the Millers' farm, but she couldn't get out the words Joseph Miller had spoken. They simply did not come. She wanted to confess to her conniving, self-centered ways, how she had gone up to talk Ruthie into giving Samuel to her. Instead she found herself seeing Joseph's shining eyes, the way they had stared at her with both honesty and love, and how they had pulled open the long-closed doors within her. And the weeping grew even stronger.

Kenneth gently led her into the living room and guided her onto the sofa. He kept her close, stroking her shoulder, her hair, her face.

Kyle forced herself to regain a semblance of control and tried once more. This time she started with the morning's visit to Abigail, and the words came easier. She stopped, her breathing shaky, but the weeping eased, and then she finished with, "I didn't have anything to give her. I could tell her the words, and I led her through a prayer. But there wasn't anything inside me. Nothing. A great big emptiness. I sat there and listened to Abigail talk about living a lie, and I felt as though I should have been the one saying all those words."

He carefully eased her back to look at her. Yet Kyle did not want to meet his gaze. She felt so ashamed. Even when one hand lifted her chin slightly, still she kept her gaze averted.

"I've pushed everything away." She forced the words out. They had to be said. She did not know why, but she was as certain of this as she was of her own mistakes. It was not enough to admit all this to herself. She had to say it. Speak the words and confess both to her husband and to God. "I've kept you out and I've kept God out. Our relationship, my relationship with God, my whole life. I've just shriveled up inside. I've been so wrong. So awful. All the things I've said, what I've done . . . oh, I just can't stand it. I can't . . ."

Kyle's bitter tears of remorse threatened to drown her in their sorrow. But Kenneth's strong arms did not let her go. He drew her up tightly once more and held her so close she could feel the good man's strength and peace reach inside and begin to fill and heal and soothe.

"Thank God," he murmured, kissing the side of her face. "Oh, thank God."

CHAPTER TWENTY-EIGHT

KYLE OPENED HER EYES in time to greet the dawn. Softly, softly, she turned and looked over at her sleeping husband. The strength in his face was solid and certain, even in repose. Such an incredible combination of strength and gentleness and patience. And forgiveness.

She lay there beside him remembering how he had listened to her and spoken with her the evening before. He had held her there on the living room sofa, cradling her with his love until she was all cried out. While she was still unable to lift her gaze, he had begun to speak. As though all this time he had been storing things up, not anger and accusations, but *wisdom*.

There had been no recriminations. None of the condemnation she knew she deserved. Instead he had talked about what he himself had learned concerning pain and loss, concerning trust in a good God to do *good*. And he had told her about the gift of peace that had come at a time when even asking for such a gift was beyond him. He talked about that experience as if it had been meant for both of them from the very beginning. And come to think of it, maybe it had.

"I felt I was descending into an abyss after little Charles died," he had softly explained to her the night before, describing his own journey. "My heart was crushed, the baby was gone, you were in such deep pain, and I was utterly helpless. Helpless and frustrated and angry. There was no hope, no purpose to life except to suffer and fail."

The words echoed inside her, giving voice to all the things she had refused to allow herself to think. She gave a quiet little sigh.

"You probably thought I was weak, that I had failed you."

"No, not at all," she whispered. "I knew, even when I didn't want to accept it, that you were so brave."

"I didn't feel brave. Many times I felt angry and defeated. Often my prayers were silent cries of hopelessness and anger. But even when I dared to accuse God, underneath it all I knew He wasn't giving up on me, or on us. Then one night . . ." He hesitated there, taking a long moment before he continued more quietly than before. "That evening after our pastor's visit when you were so angry at him, at me, and probably at God, I felt like I was standing at the edge of a chasm. One utterly dark. A void that would swallow me whole."

Kenneth's hand stopped caressing her face. His voice turned sad as he went on. "I was so tempted. I hate to say it, but that's the truth. I knew if I continued on the path I was taking, with my anger and my burning frustration, it would not matter whether we stayed together or not. It would all be lost. And the fact that you were so cold and distant made it all that much more inviting to step forward and fall into darkness. To just let it swallow me up."

Kyle wiped quickly at new tears in order to concentrate on Kenneth's words.

"I don't know what exactly happened. Well, maybe I

do. I just don't know if I can explain it. It felt as though all the years of prayer and Scripture reading had built up a reserve of strength within me, preparing me for such a moment. At least now that it's over, that's what it feels like to me. When God reached down into my heart of stone with His gift of peace, I found the ability to turn." He took a deep breath.

"It really felt like that, Kyle. Like I turned away from the darkness and the anger and the raging frustration, and I accepted the gift. The pain was still with me. I think a part of me will always ache for little Charles. Strange how a baby who was with us for such a short while could become such a part of me. I think . . ." He stopped to gather himself with an effort that firmed the arms holding her close. "I think maybe we each gave a part of our hearts, our souls, to the little baby while he was still inside you. And when he went up to heaven, it felt like he took that part of our hearts away with him."

She had to move back then, move far enough from within his embrace so she could look at his face. She wanted to tell him how beautiful that thought was, how restoring, even when it hurt so. But she did not want to distract him from all she saw still unfinished in his eyes.

"I made the turning. And I knew God would be there, waiting for me. There was no thunderbolt or words from on high. Just a peace, Kyle. Even when I had felt as though my very soul was shriveled inside me, the peace filled me. And I knew it wasn't mine. It was God's. And I knew right then that everything was going to be all right. No matter how bad things seemed, how bleak. He would see us—both of us—through this."

She wanted to hold him, to kiss him, and to beg his forgiveness. Tell him just how much it meant to have such a wonderful man. How she did not deserve him, but that she wanted to love him and fill all their remaining days with a new union. A stronger one, forged by the fires of life, bonded together closer than ever.

But again she did not speak. The need to say something more was there in his gaze.

"I discovered something in those following days," Kenneth said. "I learned that if I allowed my faith to be moved this way and that by the circumstances of life, then I was standing too far from God. If I was thinking that having good things and a good life meant being blessed by God, and that bad things meant abandonment by God, then I did not have a real faith. Not the faith that Jesus lived and died for me to have."

Kyle nodded. She was guilty. But at that same moment she knew with a certainty that flooded her heart that she was not just guilty. She was *forgiven*. She turned her face to Kenneth's with a joy that filled her being.

"God has not deserted us," she heard him continue. "He has been with us through it all—even when we weren't aware of it. Maybe even when we were aware of it but didn't want to be. His promise is that He will be with us from the first day to the last. In the pain, in the joy. He is here, Kyle. He is here."

Kyle leaned back, pulling his arms from around her, holding his hands with both of hers. Looking at him, she whispered, "Would you pray with me?"

Kenneth stirred. Kyle leaned over and softly kissed his lips.

"Good morning, my beloved," he whispered.

"I love you, my husband."

He nodded. She knew that he knew.

After another kiss, she murmured, "I need to see someone this morning. But first I am going to serve you breakfast in bed."

CHAPTER TWENTY-NINE

KYLE STEPPED ONTO THE small front porch, raised her hand to knock on the door, then hesitated. She brought the hand back to her mouth and stood there a long moment. She then straightened her shoulders, took a breath, and knocked.

Martha Grimes opened the door, her eyes round with astonishment. "Kyle!"

"Hello . . . hello, Mother." A great lump of sorrow threatened to close her throat up before she had even started. Kyle swallowed with difficulty. "Am I disturbing you? May I come in?"

"Of course you're not. And of course you can." Martha's smile was tremulous as she pushed the door fully open. "I'm so happy to see you."

"And surprised, I know." After so long, she had to be. Kyle stepped into the cramped front room. "Is . . . is Dad here?"

"No, he had an errand downtown." Martha seemed at a loss to know what to do or say. "Would you like a cup of coffee?" Martha drew her across the room to two chairs close together.

"No, thank you. Not today. But I do want to talk with you," Kyle said as they sat down. She stopped and took another breath. "I want you to know how sorry I am for the way I've treated you."

Martha's eyes filled with tears. "Kyle, dear, you don't need to apologize."

"Yes, I do," Kyle hurried on, pinching one hand with the other as she tried to keep her composure. "I was horrible. To you, to Kenneth, to Dad, to everybody."

"You were not horrible, Kyle. You were afraid."

Kyle looked into Martha's face for a moment, then nodded slowly.

"Yes, I was afraid. I've spent a lot of time these past few days thinking about what you said when you came over to visit me. It was just after Joel and Ruthie's baby was born. Do you remember?"

Martha bit her lip and gave a jerky little nod.

"You said that I needed to let God in, and let Him help me. And you were right. I had been doing exactly what you said, trying to lock everything up inside, and shut God and everyone else out."

Martha reached out a hand. "Oh, Kyle honey."

"I've caused the people I love the most in the world so much pain," Kyle said around a sob. Then she held out her arms.

Martha and Kyle embraced each other with a fierceness that seemed to pull down all the walls between them, all the time, all the distance. Martha whispered, "It's going to be all right."

Kyle let the tears flow. She knew what Martha said was true. It was all right. And it was going to stay that way.

"Kyle!" Reverend Patrick Langdon rose quickly to his feet. "Goodness, how long have you been standing there?"

"Not long. May I come in?"

"Of course. Here, take this seat." He pulled another chair up close to hers and seated himself without taking his eyes from her face. "Kyle, I am very glad to see you."

"Thank you." His genuine warmth after her behavior toward him brought a faint blush to her cheeks. "It is good to see you again."

"How are you?" His smile hinted at more than social courtesy.

"I'm fine. Really." She cocked her head. "Why are you smiling?"

"Oh, nothing. Well, yes, it is something, I suppose. I was thinking it is the first time in a long while I can ask you that question and look forward to what you have to say."

"Yes. Yes, that's true." She looked down at her hands. "God has been working in me. And Kenneth has helped. Actually, God has used many people to get my attention and point me back to Him. Including you."

"I'm glad," he said simply.

"I truly am sorry for my rudeness to you," she said, her voice low.

"Kyle, don't even think about it again. I won't." And his warm smile told her even more than his words.

She knew he had a hundred questions, but he only said, "What can I do for you?"

"I need to ask a favor." Kyle opened her purse and extracted an envelope. "I want you to give this to Ruthie."

He accepted it, then looked at her with a question in his eyes.

"It's some money, and it needs to be an anonymous gift. I don't want her to know it's come from me. If she knew, she might not . . ." A shadow came and went across her features, like clouds pushed by an invisible wind. "Tell her it is for her and Samuel, that she can't spend it only on the mission. She probably will anyway, but tell her that it's designated for her and for Samuel."

He looked from the envelope to her and back again.

"It comes from dividends on Daddy's stock," she explained.

"Your stock," he noted quietly. "Your father left the shares to you."

Kyle nodded and rose to her feet. "I have to be going. It took longer at the bank than I thought, and I need to get to the post office before it closes." She hesitated, then straightened her shoulders and said determinedly, "I have a letter to write."

"Ruthie will be delighted." Patrick walked over and offered Kyle his hand. "As for myself, I can't tell you how nice it is to see you smile again."

She turned for the door. "We'll see you on Sunday."

The morning was still young, still holding to the hint of spring freshness. May was a time of transition for farmers, spring in the morning and summer by midafternoon. Joseph Miller was seated in his padded chair on the corner of the porch, watching and listening to the birth of a new day. He missed helping with the morning chores, but still he felt a part of the daily activities. His heart pulsed in time to the farm. It was in his veins.

"Papa?" Sarah came across the porch. "Here's a letter for you."

"Thank you, kinder."

The girl handed him a kitchen knife along with the envelope. "Mama says breakfast will be in fifteen minutes."

"Good, good. I will be there." But the return address was already holding his attention. He slit the envelope with the knife and extracted the letter. A slender slip of paper fluttered down to lie upon his shortened leg.

Slowly, slowly, he reached down beside his leg and picked up the slip of paper. His hand trembled as he held it up close, wanting to be sure of what he was seeing.

He unfolded the letter. He stopped to take a breath, then read the first page, turned it over, and had to stop again. Joseph Miller wiped his eyes, then started on the second page.

When he was finished he looked out over the farm for a long moment. Then he called out, "Simon!"

"I'm with the chickens, Papa."

"Leave the eggs for later. Come here with you right now!"

There was the clatter of a pail, and Simon came running from the chicken house. "What's wrong?"

"Nothing. Nothing is wrong." Joseph's answer was loud enough to bring Ruth and Sarah through the front door.

His wife inspected his face. "Why do you make such a fuss on this peaceful morning?"

Joseph kept his gaze on his son. "How much land do you plan for the flowers?"

Simon exchanged a glance with his mother and sister. "But the money—"

"How much land?" Joseph quietly demanded.

"Four acres, Papa."

"Flowers are a new crop for us. We do not know how much water they will need. Take those down by the stream."

"But, Papa," Simon and his sister said in unison. Then

Simon finished, "Four acres means sixty thousand plants."

"Then you best be ordering them, and seeing to some extra hands for the planting," Joseph replied. He looked at his wife and asked, "Are you to the market this morning?"

"It's Thursday." Ruth stared at her husband in wide-eyed disbelief. "I always go on Thursday."

"I believe I will travel with you. I have some business at the bank. Together we will stop off by the Brueder place on the way home." Joseph Miller allowed his smile to surface as he waved the check at them. "We have ourselves a wedding to plan."

CHAPTER THIRTY

KYLE SAT AT THE KITCHEN TABLE gazing out the back window. The clock above the stove ticked loudly in the quiet room. She had been home for over an hour, and still she had not managed to take off her coat.

She glanced at the phone on the cabinet wall and knew she should call Kenneth. But she could not seem to find the strength to rise. Crossing the floor and picking up the phone and forming the words to tell him—it was all too difficult. She could see him now, rushing back, listening to the news, and then sweeping her up in his arms. But she could not start the process in motion.

"It can't be," she whispered for the hundredth time. "It just can't be true."

But even as she fought against it, inwardly she knew it was true. Even without the doctor's confirmation, she knew.

The whispers kept coming, the quiet little protests. "But how can we have another child? Not after . . ."

Fear gripped her heart. What if it happened again? What if she bore another child with a damaged heart? *What if she lost another baby?*

The thought stabbed at her heart with lances of fear. She could not go through it again.

Kyle caught the faintest hint of another voice—a still, quiet voice, one almost lost amid her inner storm. Straining to hear the soft words brought her a first ray of hope. *"He is here, Kyle—He is here,"* she heard as she remembered her husband's declaration.

Kyle yearned to accept the truth, but her mind shouted back, *God allowed my first baby to die.*

She found herself listening to the first voice. *And yet He was there. I survived.*

"I didn't want to. For months I didn't want to," she argued aloud.

But I did. And over the past few weeks, since she and Kenneth had come back to each other, she had discovered a new strength of faith.

But would she be strong enough to face the loss of another baby?

Kyle knotted her hands together in her lap and bowed her head. The words seemed to rise up from the deepest part of her being, forcing their way through the storm in her mind. "Lord, I need your help. I need you," Kyle whispered. "I'm so frightened. I don't want to go through what I went through before. If another baby is on the way, you will have to walk with me the whole way, Lord. I must lean on you. Help me to trust you completely—whatever happens."

Kyle heard little paws tap their way lightly across the kitchen floor. She felt the nuzzling of Goldie's wet nose against her leg. Instinctively her hand patted the small dog's head. A soft whine started somewhere deep within the spaniel's chest, and she pressed closer to Kyle's skirt.

Kyle opened her eyes and stroked the fur around Goldie's ears. "I wish I could trust as simply as you can," she whispered. "My Master is far more trustworthy than your mistress is. I need to let go of my concerns and let God take care of me. And of the baby."

She found herself listening to the words as though they were being spoken by someone else. "What has happened in the past has no bearing on the promises of the future. He has said He will be with me. That is a promise. He never breaks His promises. Even if it means . . ."

Yes, it was true. She could trust. She would have to trust. And though Kyle inwardly trembled when thinking of the future, she felt a gentle assurance that indeed she could lean on her Lord.

Kyle lifted the puppy to her lap. The little dog responded by nuzzling her delightedly. She smiled, rose and tucked Goldie under her arm, and crossed the kitchen to the phone. She picked up the receiver and dialed Kenneth's number.

He would be so overjoyed.

CHAPTER THIRTY-ONE

KYLE REACHED FOR ABIGAIL'S ARM as they moved away from the taxi. They were still four blocks from the mission, but she had not minded when her mother had asked the driver to drop them off here. The day was lovely and warm, and the doctor encouraged her to walk as much as possible. "Thank you so much for coming with me today," she said to Abigail as she squeezed her arm.

"I would not have missed this for the world." Abigail drew the hand up close. "As a matter of fact, I asked the taxi to let us off here so I could say something. I've been wanting to talk with you for some time now, but I just couldn't seem to find the words."

Kyle glanced at her mother. The previous four months had made a remarkable transformation in her. Or rather, God had worked the transformation.

On the outside Abigail remained much the same. She dressed impeccably, not a hair was out of place, and she walked with such poise and confidence that most people could not help but pause and look her way. Yet the inward change was clearly evident. Her eyes shone with a new calm light, the same light which radiated from her features.

Kyle believed her mother was truly happy for the first time in her life.

"The day I bought Goldie for you, do you remember that?"

"Of course." Kyle could not repress a smile at the thought of the curious little dog. "When I think back about it, the day Goldie arrived was when something inside me opened up to the light."

"It was a day of opening up for me as well," Abigail said ruefully. "I realized then just how false and superficial my life had always been."

"Mother—"

"No, let me finish, Kyle. It was only after I realized how shallow my life had been, how empty my answers and my promises, that I could begin to feel a need for something else, something deeper."

Abigail stopped so she could look directly at her daughter. She reached over and grasped Kyle's other hand. "And it was you who showed me the truth."

"Me? But I was caught up in living the same lie, feeling I had to be in control—"

"Exactly. You were becoming what I had always wanted you to be, and what I knew then was so wrong. For both of us." Abigail looked stricken with grief. "Oh, Kyle, I pushed you to be something, someone, you were not. I made your childhood a misery."

A tear escaped and rolled down Abigail's cheek. Kyle felt a burning in her own eyes but did not want to release Abigail to wipe it away. Abigail took a shaky breath and said, "I just wanted to apologize. To put into words how wrong I was to demand and to cause you such pain. And how right you were to refuse."

Kyle managed to whisper, "You don't need—"

"Yes, I most certainly do. You showed me how wrong

I had always been by finally doing what I had always wanted. Your pain pushed you into seeking superficial answers to life, but I don't have that excuse. I did it because I wanted to control everything, especially my life. I refused to see anything beyond my own desires. I lived my life on the shallowest possible level."

Kyle squeezed both her hands. "Not anymore."

"No, thanks to you."

"And God."

"Yes." Abigail's face crumpled as she wept. "Oh, Kyle, can you forgive me?"

Kyle smiled through her own tears as their arms encircled each other. She whispered, "There is nothing left to forgive."

Ruthie cautiously agreed to the visit when Kyle called. Uneasy memories of their encounter at the mission were still with her. Even after receiving Kyle's letter of apology, Ruthie wasn't quite sure of what she should expect. Kyle explained that she had chosen to contact her by letter to save Ruthie the awkwardness of attempting to forgive her on the spot.

Kyle was scarcely in the door when Ruthie heard her exclaim, "Look how big he's grown!"

To her surprise, Abigail joined her in the doorway, "And he's brown as a berry!"

Ruthie stood back and let the two women bend down to admire the sturdy little boy. He responded with a one-tooth grin and a very wet coo. Ruthie said, "Soon enough he's going to be into everything."

"I can't believe how much he's changed just in these

last months. He's not an infant anymore," Kyle said, joining the baby on the floor. "You're growing up so fast. Aren't you, yes?" Kyle reached out, and Samuel grasped her finger with a chubby hand.

"I'm with him every day, and still I can't believe how fast he changes." Ruthie remained cautious in her inspection of Kyle. She had seen Kyle at church a few times, but this was her first chance since the spring to have a good long look at Kyle with the baby.

As she watched, the painful memories and the concerns she had felt since Kyle had telephoned began to evaporate. Kyle was not just playing at happiness. It was coming from deep inside. The baby knew it, too, and responded to her cooing and hand games with delighted chuckles. Ruthie felt her tension drain away. It was true. Kyle was back with them again.

"You look . . . you look lovely," Ruthie said softly.

"Doesn't she just," Abigail agreed, rising to her feet.

Ruthie had also seen Abigail several times over the past few months at church, where she had made a point of coming over, talking and getting to know the baby. Trying to forge bonds which still astonished and moved Ruthie. Now she walked over and gave Ruthie a big hug. "You are as healthy looking and tanned as your baby."

"That's what farm life will do for you," Ruthie joked, then added, "Samuel loves our visits home."

Kyle raised her head to give them both a smile. There was so much heart in it, such a sense of warmth and concern and deep joy that Ruthie felt tears spring to her eyes.

"Samuel and I go up to the farm as often as we can," Ruthie explained. "They've needed every hand they could spare, first getting the flowers into the earth and then harvesting the blooms. Not only that, but the summer's been so hot, and this city air is probably not good for the baby.

It's the only thing that makes me wish I wasn't here working in the mission. It means that Samuel has to live in a place where there's so little green."

She dropped down to her knees, more to see Kyle's face up close than because she wanted to be near her son. She watched as Kyle and Abigail exchanged a glance. Ruthie turned to look up at the older woman's face, but found only pride and that same quiet satisfaction. Ruthie went on. "Then we had to start picking the wild flowers. I've been tying little Samuel to my back and carrying him along."

"It looks like he's enjoyed it."

"He loves every minute out there," Ruthie agreed. "He chatters to the butterflies and the clouds, and when he gets tired he just falls asleep." She stretched a hand toward Samuel, and he grabbed at it playfully. "The wild flowers have their own seasons, and we have to be there and ready when they bloom. Let's see, we've been gathering baby's breath and larkspur and straw flowers. Then we walk the gravelly river bottoms looking for pussy willows and wormwood and sage. We use them because they keep their fragrance a long time. You have to be careful, though. Have your mouth open when you pick it and you'll taste nothing but sage for the rest of the day."

Kyle used one hand to keep the baby occupied, playing like a little creeping animal that finally raced up and tickled the baby's stomach. Samuel loved it and punctuated their communication with squeals of laughter.

"Simon set up rafters in the larger barn," Ruthie went on. "We're turning it into the drying shed. Four acres doesn't sound like much, but all the plants have to be harvested by hand so the flowers aren't damaged."

"Four acres sound like an enormous amount to me," Abigail responded, smiling down at Samuel. "Are you sure you can sell them all?"

"We've already had a company meet with us, and they want to buy everything we can give them. Simon and Papa talked and talked about this. They decided to give them half, enough to cover all our costs and pay for next year's planting. The rest we'll sell ourselves in the winter markets. Simon says we can get a lot more selling directly to customers, and Sarah loves to design the arrangements in the holders. You should see what they're collecting—old toolboxes, rusty cans, cracked flowerpots, creamers, egg crates, broken baskets from other farms, even an old bird-house."

"You sound like you don't quite believe it all," Kyle observed.

"Part of me doesn't," Ruthie agreed, with a little laugh. "After all the problems and worries at the farm, it's hard to imagine we might have it all behind us. And now Simon's getting married in the fall. . . ." She shook her head. "And the money for the flowers. Where did it come from? It seems like a miracle."

There was a moment's silence before Abigail said quietly, "Yes. Yes, that is exactly what we have seen. All of us. A true miracle."

Ruthie caught sight of another glance between mother and daughter. One so full of joy and love she felt as though any further question no longer mattered.

Abigail turned her smile to Ruthie and announced, "Kyle has some news of her own."

"So do you," Kyle countered.

"I would rather you tell her that as well," Abigail replied.

"Mother . . ."

"Please, Kyle. For me."

"All right." A smile sparkled over Kyle's features. "Then you tell her the other part."

"Come on, you two!" Ruthie laughed. "Somebody tell me *something!*"

Abigail turned to Ruthie, took a big breath, and announced, "Samuel is going to have a cousin."

Ruthie took only a moment to figure it out. "Oh, Kyle!" Her own heart leaped with joy. "This is wonderful!"

"Almost four months," Kyle said, rising so she could accept Ruthie's hug. "I didn't want to believe it at first, and then I was afraid to tell anyone."

Ruthie nodded in understanding. "And now?"

"Now," Kyle said, taking a long breath, "now I am learning to put my trust in God. Kenneth reminds me. And Abigail. And Martha and Harry. I don't know what I'd do without them."

"I'm so glad you told me," Ruthie said warmly. "Now I can add my prayers to theirs. Each and every day."

"Thank you," Kyle said, and once more they hugged.

"Now tell her the other part," Abigail urged.

"Won't you do it?" Kyle asked shyly.

"You promised."

"All right." Another breath, then she began. "Mother decided she wanted to sell the house."

"It's too big for one person," Abigail added. "It's too big for one family, for that matter. It's huge."

Kyle looked at her. "Are you sure you don't want to tell her?"

"You're doing fine." Abigail waved her hands and motioned for Kyle to continue.

Kyle turned back to Ruthie. "I'd be sorry to see it go. I was raised there. And now it's the place where I remember my father the most clearly."

"I'm amazed to hear her say this," Abigail told Ruthie. "She was never happy there." Her tone acknowledged her sorrow for Kyle's lost childhood.

"There were some nice times," Kyle said quietly. "Maggie and Bertrand were good to me. And old Jim. And I met my husband there."

"Well, now it has all the heart and soul of a museum," Abigail explained. "I rattle around those huge old rooms and get lost if I'm not careful."

Kyle looked at her mother. "I thought you didn't want to tell this."

"I'm just helping with a few details," Abigail said. "You go ahead."

"All right." A pause, then, "We have been thinking we could make it into apartments. At least three of them. One for Abigail, one for me and Kenneth, and one . . ." Kyle drifted to a stop, took a quick look at Ruthie, then looked at Samuel.

"You just said the baby needs to be around some green," Kyle went on in a rush. "This place has acres of lawn for him to play in. And Abigail could help look after him when you're down working at the mission."

"Not to mention that Harry and Martha live not too far away," Abigail added. "Or maybe we could convince them to let me renovate the gardener's cottage for them. It hasn't been lived in since Old Jim retired. With a new conservatory and a large upper story added, I'm sure it would make a lovely place for them."

"But don't say anything yet to them," Kyle added hastily. "We didn't want to speak with them until we'd heard what you think of the idea." She reached over and took Ruthie's hand. "It would be so nice to see us gather together as a family. And Samuel and our . . . our baby can be playmates."

Ruthie felt their eyes on her. She stammered, "I . . . I just don't know what to say."

"There's something else, and this I will say for her."

Abigail looked at her daughter with loving concern. "Having a youngster around will help Kyle immensely. And having you nearby, Ruthie, will also help continue the healing. . . ."

Abigail did not finish the thought. She did not need to. Ruthie watched as Kyle turned and looked at Samuel, and in that instant the answer came to her heart. There in Kyle's look at her son was everything she needed to know.

No longer desperation, or grasping, or manipulation. Only love and friendship. Ruthie said, "I would love to. This is an answer to my prayers."

CHAPTER THIRTY-TWO

HER CRY OF FEAR SIGNALED the nightmare's release. She awoke gasping for air.

Kenneth was instantly awake and reaching for her. "It's all right, honey."

"Oh, Kenneth, it . . . it was the dream again."

"I know, I know, but that is all it was." He sat up so he could cradle her with one arm. "Only a dream."

For an instant, she was gripped by a powerful temptation to give in to the dark fears and the old feelings. But it was merely the last tendrils of the nightmare. She willed herself to relax into his embrace, letting him be strong for her, taking his confidence and his love and his peace and making it her own. "I was so afraid," she murmured into his chest.

"I know, honey." Not masking it, nor making light of it. Just being there, helping her through the dark moments, sharing both the joy and the heartache. "Would you like to pray?"

"You say the words." She closed her eyes and listened as he asked for the Lord's peace and confidence to fill them. But in truth she was feeling more than hearing, letting the last whispers of nighttime dreads be swept away.

She opened her eyes to find Kenneth watching her. She confessed, "I was dreaming about little Charles."

Kenneth did not speak. She knew he understood.

"But the pain was . . . was a clean pain. That probably doesn't make any sense, but that's how it felt."

"It does make sense," Kenneth said quietly.

"I know the doctor says everything seems fine." Fear turned her so weak she had to draw away from him in order to continue. "But sometimes it just, I don't know . . ."

"All the past rises up and leaves you afraid."

She looked at him in desperate appeal. "Do you really believe this baby will be all right? Do you?"

"I hope so. I pray so. That is all we can do." He stroked her hair. "We pray that whatever happens, we will find our way through together. With God's help."

"With God's help," she agreed tremulously. "Oh, Kenneth, I don't know what I'd do without you." She felt a pang as she remembered all that had happened in the past year. "I'm so sorry—"

He stopped her with a single finger to her lips and a smile that warmed her and filled her heart. "Yes, I know."

She sighed her way back onto her pillow, loving him. Yes, whatever happened. With God's help.

She sat down by the small suitcase in the front hallway. She started to call to Kenneth but decided there was no need to rush him. Let him finish dressing and come down at his own pace. The morning would be fraught with enough hurry and tension for both of them without calling out now. Besides, she wanted to have a moment here by herself.

The tall hall mirror was directly across from where she sat in the high-backed chair. Kyle gave her reflection a frank inspection. There was fear in her eyes, certainly. And anticipation. But there was also peace. It gave her great assurance to see that in her eyes, to recognize it with an honesty that she knew came from beyond herself. She knew she was not alone. No matter what came, no matter what happened, she would face it with her Lord. And her husband. And her family.

And Goldie. The small dog padded down the hall and sat, as she usually did, so she could lean against Kyle's right leg. She was growing into a beautiful spaniel. And she was such a good friend. Kyle dropped her hand to the bright head and asked Goldie about the morning's weather. Goldie tipped her head and listened solemnly, only her tail twitching with her enthusiasm for life.

She seemed to catch Kyle's mood and laid her head on Kyle's knee. The chocolate eyes watched her calmly, as the clock on the living room mantel clicked steadily onward. Kyle rested her other hand on her abdomen and listened to the ticking sound and the sense of the future unfolding around her. She did not know what was coming. But knowing that she entered into it with God's love in and around her gave her the strength to be calm. Even here. Even now.

Kyle bowed her head. Her words were few. She sensed with a crystal clarity that the Lord already knew.

The sound of Kenneth descending the stairs lifted her head. He was still knotting his tie, but the instant he caught sight of her face, he stopped midstep.

She gave him a little smile and said, "It's time."

CHAPTER THIRTY-THREE

KENNETH SAT IN THE HALL leading from the delivery room to the main ward. He felt as though all his muscles had given way. He watched Harry approach, knowing he should say something. But simply drawing breath took every bit of strength he had left.

One glance at Kenneth's face seemed to be enough for Harry to understand. He sat down beside his son-in-law and placed a hand on his shoulder. The two men sat there for a long moment in silence.

Thoughts jumbled upon one another in Kenneth's mind as he tried to find some way to express what he was feeling. How much their walks and talks had meant to him, how close he felt to Harry at this moment. But he simply could not find the words.

It was Harry who finally spoke, his voice quiet and shaky. "I've been meaning to tell you this for some time now. But talking never has come naturally to me. It's been easier to stay silent than speak. But I can't do that anymore."

A long sigh seemed to force open the door within him, and Harry continued, "Back after I got home from the war,

I found myself hurt more by my baby girl's absence than from my battle wounds. The inner part took a lot longer to heal, too. Years and years. Not until I found God was I able to cast aside all the anger and the hurt and the bitterness." He was silent a moment, then added quietly, "And all the pain I caused my family."

"Harry——"

"Hang on now, just let me get this out. When your baby died and you two were staring your own sadness in the face, I felt as though all the years had been peeled back and I was going to have to live through it all, right over again. It hurt me so bad, I can't tell you how tough it was to stand there and see you two in pain, and not have a thing I could do."

The silence seemed to reach out from them, taking in the hall and the ward and the hospital beyond. Not even the rushing, clattering activity could breach the power of that quiet moment. Harry went on, "The only thing I could do was pray. Pray for you two to find your way out, pray for me to be there and help in whatever way I could."

"You helped," Kenneth managed to say. "You're helping now. More than you could ever know."

"That's good. Real good. Because I found for myself that even though I couldn't do the healing for you, I could give what God gave to me. I could love you two. . . ." He had to stop then, gathering himself with one long breath before he could continue. "Love you as God has loved me. Show you the concern and the strength He has given me. I'm sorry you two had to endure what you have. But I want to tell you how close I feel I've come to you, as though loving you two has taught me how to love God, and praying for your healing and peace has brought a deeper peace into my own life."

Harry stopped then and stared down at his hands. "I haven't said that well."

"Oh but you have," Kenneth said slowly. "You've said it wonderfully."

"I feel like God has given me a new family," Harry said. "A new son and a daughter I never deserved. And now—"

"Mr. Adams?" The nurse walked over to stand by Kenneth. "Dr. Pearce is ready for you."

Kenneth and Harry jumped to their feet at the same instant. Kenneth felt his heart constrict. "Is everything. . . ?"

The nurse smiled. "Let's wait and have the doctor give you the news."

The sounds of the maternity ward surrounded Kyle as she lay in the hospital bed. She strained to hear the footsteps that paused at her door. And then Kenneth and Dr. Pearce came hurrying into the room. As soon as she caught sight of the two faces, she raised both hands to her mouth. She knew before either of them said a word.

In a voice lacking his normal fatigue, even though he had been awake all night, Dr. Pearce declared, "She is fine. Has a perfect heart."

Kyle closed her eyes just for an instant—she had to share this with the Lord. *Her heart is fine*, she told Him silently, as if He didn't know. The tears flowed freely down her cheeks. *Oh, thank you, Father. Thank you. Her heart is fine.*

She lifted her head and her eyes locked with Kenneth's. The tears were running down his cheeks as well. She reached out to him at the same time that he moved to embrace her.

"She's fine," she heard him whisper, his voice choked. "Her heart is fine."

Kyle's heart swelled with love and gratitude. Her mind rang with the thought that God was real. *God is here. God is forgiving.* She could feel Him with her in the room and sense His love. Not just because of their baby, but for many, many more reasons.

A new realization swept through her. Her bitterness and resentment were gone, entirely gone. Even the fear had left her. She had to stop and marvel a moment, there with her arms still wrapped around her husband. Her tears began again as she realized with utter certainty that even if the baby had not been healthy and whole, she still would have made it through the ordeal without giving up her faith. God was God, and He was with her.

As her arms tightened about Kenneth's neck, she whispered to him with such joy that it made her tremble, "My heart is fine, too. Just fine."

"Mrs. Adams?" A woman's voice caused Kyle to release her husband and look up.

The nurse stood beside the bed, smiling and holding a little bundle toward her. "Would you like to hold your daughter?"

Kyle looked at the tiny face topped with dark hair, at the blue eyes peeking from the pink blanket. The small mouth puckered searchingly. Kyle felt a wave of love wash through her entire being. Her baby. Hers and Kenneth's. Their beautiful, healthy baby girl.

"Oh yes," she said as she held out her arms. "Come see your mama, Abigail Martha."